Richard Bach is the author of eleven books, including the multi-million selling *Jonathan Livingston Seagull*, loved around the world by three generations. *Out of My Mind*, *A Gift of Wings* and *The Bridge Across Forever* are all available as Pan paperbacks. Richard Bach lives in Washington on the United States west coast.

one

Richard Bach

a novel

PAN BOOKS

First published 1988 in the United States of America
by Silver Arrow Books, William Morrow and Co. Inc.

First published in Great Britain 1989 by Pan Books
an imprint of Macmillan Publishers Ltd
25 Eccleston Place, London SW1W 9NF
Basingstoke and Oxford
Associated companies throughout the world
www.macmillan.com

ISBN 0 330 31173 5

23 25 27 29 28 26 24

A CIP catalogue record for this book is available
from the British Library.

Printed and bound in Great Britain by
Mackays of Chatham plc, Chatham, Kent

with Leslie

We've come a long way, haven't we?

When we met twenty-five years ago, I was an airplane pilot entranced by flight, looking for meanings behind instruments and airspeeds. Twenty years ago our journey led us to a pattern of life in a seagull's wing. Ten years ago we met the saviour of the world, found out he was us. Yet for all you knew, I was a solitary soul with a mind full of headings and altitudes hidden behind a screen of words. And you were right.

At last I trusted that I knew you well enough to suggest that my adventures might have been yours also, happy ones and not-so-happy. You're beginning to understand how the world works? So am I. You've been restless and alone with what you've learned? Me, too. You've searched your life long for one dear love? I've done that as well, and found her, and in *The Bridge Across Forever*, I introduced you to my wife, Leslie Parrish-Bach.

We write together now, Leslie and I. We've become RiLeschardlie, no longer knowing where one of us ends and the other begins.

Because of *Bridge*, our family of readers has grown ever warmer. Added to the adventurers who flew with me in earlier books are those who yearn for love and those who've found it—our lives a mirror of theirs, they write, over and again. Could it be that we all are changed, reflecting each other?

We usually read our mail in the kitchen, one reading aloud while the other fixes the surprise meal of the day. We've laughed so with some readers' letters that salads have spilled into our soup; others have given us tears for salt.

One day, for ice, came this one:

> Remember the alternate Richard you wondered about in *Bridge*, the one who ran away, who refused to trade his many women for Leslie? I thought you'd want to hear from me because I'm that man, and I know what happened next.

The parallels he told us were astonishing. He, too, is a writer, had earned a sudden fortune from one book, had fallen into the same tax troubles that I had. He, too, had stopped searching for one woman and settled for many.

12

Then he'd met the one who loved him for who he was, and in time she had given him a choice: she'd be the only woman in his life or she'd not be in his life at all. It was the same choice that Leslie once had given me; he had stood at the same fork in the road.

At the fork I had turned left, to choose intimacy and the warm future I hoped might come with it.

He had turned right. He had flown away from the woman who loved him, had left his home and airplane for the tax collector to seize and had fled, as I nearly had, to New Zealand. He went on:

> ... the writing is going well, I have houses in Auckland and Madrid and Singapore, I can travel everywhere in the world except the United States. No one gets too close to me.
>
> But I still think about my Laura. I wonder what would have happened if I had given her a chance. Does *Bridge* tell me? Are you two still together? Did I make the right choice? Did you?

The man is a multimillionaire, his wishes come true, the world is his playground. But I had to brush a tear from my eye, and looked up from his letter to find Leslie leaning against the counter, her face buried in her hands.

For so long we had thought he was fiction, a shadow-soul living out on some queer dimension in might-have-been, someone we'd invented. After his letter, we felt unsettled, uneasy, as if a bell were ringing for us and we didn't know how to answer.

Then, coincidence, I read an odd little book of physics: *The*

Many-Worlds Interpretation of Quantum Mechanics. Many worlds indeed, it says. Every instant the world we know splits into an infinite number of other worlds, different futures and different pasts.

According to physics, the Richard who chose to run away did not vanish at the crossroads where I changed my life. He exists this moment in an alternate world sliding alongside this one. In that world, Leslie Parrish chose a different life as well: Richard Bach is not her husband, he's a man she let go when she found it was not love and joy he offered, but endless sorrow.

After *Many Worlds,* my subconscious took a ghost-copy of the book to bed, read it every night, nudged me as I slept.

What if you could find a way into those parallel worlds, it whispered. What if you could meet the Richard and Leslie you were before you made your worst mistakes and smartest moves? What if you could warn them, thank them, ask them any question you dared? What might they know about living, about youth and age and dying, career and love and country, about peace and war, responsibility, choices and consequences, about the world you think is real?

Go away, I said.

You think you don't belong in this world with its wars and destruction, its hatred and violence? Why do you live here?

Let me sleep, I said.

Good night, it said.

But ghost-minds never sleep, and I heard pages turning in my dreams.

I'm awake now, and the questions remain. Do our choices really change our worlds? What if science turns out to be true?

We slanted down from the north in our snow-and-rainbow sea-plane, over mountains the color of old memory. The vast concrete waffle of the city rose ahead of us from the haze, baking in summer, end-of-the-line dessert after a long flight.

"How far, sweetie?" I said on the interphone.

Leslie touched the long-range navigation receiver and numbers glowed on the instrument panel. "Thirty-two miles north," she said, "fifteen minutes out. Do you want L.A. Approach?"

"Thank you," I said, and smiled. How much we had changed since we had found each other! She, once terrified of flying, now a pilot herself. I, once terrified of marriage, now husband of eleven years and still feeling like a lucky date.

"Hi, Los Angeles Approach," I said to the microphone, "this is Martin Seabird One Four Bravo with you out of seven-thousand-five for three-thousand-five, southbound to Santa Monica." Between us we called our seaplane *Growly*; to Air Traffic Control we gave the official title.

How is it we're the lucky ones, I thought, living a life that the children-we-were took for dreams? In half a century of challenge and learning and trial-and-error, each of us had struggled from hard times to a present lovely beyond our dreams.

"Martin One Four Bravo is radar contact," came the voice in our headphones.

"Traffic there," said Leslie, "and there."

"Got 'em in sight." I looked at her, too, actress turned partner in adventure: golden hair swept around the smooth curves of her face catching sunlight and shadow, seablue eyes all business, checking the sky around us. What a lovely face that mind had built!

"Martin One Four Bravo," said Los Angeles Approach, "squawk four six four five."

What were the odds that we would find each other, this one remarkable woman and I, that our paths would meet and match as they had? What the odds that we'd change from strangers to soulmates?

Now we flew together to Spring Hill, a meeting of researchers exploring the edges of creative thought: science and consciousness, war and peace, the future of a planet.

"Wasn't that for us?" Leslie asked.

"Right you are," I said. "What number did he say?"

She turned to me, eyes filled with amusement. "Don't you remember?" she said.

"Four six four five."

"There," she said. "What would you do without me?"

Those were the last words I heard before the world changed.

2

The radar transponder is a black box on the amphibian's instrument panel, with windows to show a four-number code. Set numbers in those windows and miles away in darkened rooms we're identified: airplane number, heading, altitude, speed — all that matters to air traffic controllers in their green-radar workplace.

That afternoon, for perhaps the ten thousandth time in my flying career, I reached to change those numbers in their windows: 4 in the first window, 6 in the second, 4 in the next, 5 in the last. While I was still looking down, focused on this task, there was a queer hum that started low C and ran straight up the scale beyond hearing, then a whomp as though we had hit a hard updraft, a crackling flash of amber light in the cockpit.

Leslie screamed. *"RICHARD!"*

I jerked my head around to see her face, mouth open, eyes wide. "A little turbulence, sweetie," I said, "some rough ai. . ."

Then I could see for myself, and stopped midword.

Los Angeles had disappeared.

Gone the horizon-wide city ahead, gone the mountains that surrounded it, gone the hundred-mile veil of haze.

Vanished.

The sky had snapped blue the color of wildflowers, deep and fresh and cold. Below were not freeways and housetops and shopping centers but unbroken sea, a mirror of the sky. Pansy-blue, that sea, not midocean deeps but all shallows, as if there were level cobalt sand one fathom down, a pattern of silvers and golds.

"Where's Los Angeles?" I said. "Do you see . . . ? Tell me what you see!"

"Water! We're over the ocean!" she gasped. "Richie, what happened?"

"I don't know!" I told her, blank confusion.

I checked the engine instruments, and every pointer was where it belonged. Airspeed unchanged, heading 142 degrees on the gyro compass. But now the *magnetic* compass spun idly in its case, no longer caring for north or south.

Leslie tested switches, pressed circuit breakers.

"Navigation radios are out," she said, fear catching in her throat. "They've got power, but they're not showing. . . ."

Sure enough. The navigation readouts were blank lines and OFF flags. The loran panel lit up a display we had never seen: NO POSITION.

Our minds gone blank too, we stared in astonishment.

"Did you see anything before it . . . changed?" I asked her.

"No," she said. "Yes! There was a whine, did you hear it? Then a flash of yellow light, a . . . a shock-wave going out all around us, and then it was gone, and so was everything else! *Where are we?*"

I summed up as best I knew. "The airplane's running fine except for the nav radios and loran. But the mag compass has failed . . . the only instrument in an airplane that cannot fail has failed! I don't know where we are!"

"Los Angeles Approach?" she said suddenly.

"Good!" I pressed the microphone button. "Hello Los Angeles Approach, Martin One Four Bravo."

I looked down, waiting for the reply. The sand beneath the water was etched in a vast twisting matrix, as if swirling light-beam rivers flowed there, rivulets branching uncountable tributaries, every one connected, shimmering a few feet below the surface.

"Hello L.A. Approach," I said again, "this is Martin Amphibian One Four Bravo, how d'you read?"

I turned the volume up and there was static in our speakers. The radio worked, but nobody was out there talking.

"Hi any station reading Martin Seabird One Four Bravo give us a call this frequency."

White noise. Not a word.

"I'm running out of ideas," I told her.

By instinct I urged the airplane to climb, trying for a bigger view, hoping that with altitude we could find some hint of the world we had lost.

In a few minutes we learned some odd facts: no matter how high we climbed, the altimeter didn't change—the air didn't go thinner with altitude. At what I guessed was five thousand feet the instrument still showed sea level.

The view didn't change either: mile after mile of kaleidoscope shoals, patterns never repeated, horizon everywhere the same. No mountains. No islands. No sun, no clouds, not a boat, not a living thing.

Leslie tapped the fuel gage. "We don't seem to be using any gas," she said. "Is that possible?"

"More likely the float is stuck." The engine ran fast or slow as I moved the throttle, but our fuel gage had frozen a pointer's width under half a tank.

"That's it," I told her, shaking my head. "Fuel gage failure, too. We probably have two hours' flying left, but I'd just as soon save what we've got."

She scanned the empty horizon. "Where shall we land?"

"Does it matter?" I asked.

The sea sparkled glory upward, mystifying us with its patterns.

I slid the throttle back and the flying-boat settled into a long glide. As we watched the eerie seascape on the way down, two bright paths sparkled, first twisting separately, then winding parallel with each other and finally joining. Thousands of others arched away from the two, branches in a willow forest.

There's a reason, I thought. Something made those lines. Were they lava flows? Roads underwater?

Leslie took my hand. "Richie," she said, soft and sad, "do you think we're dead? Maybe we hit something in the air, or something hit us so fast we never knew."

I'm the family expert on death and I hadn't even considered. . . . Could she be right? But what's Growly doing here? There's nothing I've read about dying that says it doesn't even change the oil pressure.

"This can't be dying!" I said. "The books say when we die there's a tunnel and light and all this incredible love, and people to meet us. . . . If we went to the trouble of dying together, two of us at once, wouldn't you think they'd find a way to meet us on time?"

"Maybe the books are wrong," she said.

We descended in silence, swept with sadness. How could the joy and promise of our lives have ended so swiftly?

"Do you feel dead?" she asked.

"No."

"Neither do I."

We flew low over the parallel channels, checking for coral heads or floating logs before we landed. Even when you're dead, you don't want to tear your airplane apart setting down on some rock.

"What a dumb way to end a lifetime!" Leslie said. "We don't even know what happened, we don't even know how we died!"

"The gold light, Leslie, the shock-wave! Could it have been a nuclear . . . ? Were we the first ones to die in the Third World War?"

She thought about it. "I don't think so. It wasn't coming toward us, it was going *away*. And we would have felt something."

We flew in silence. Sad. So sad.

"It's not fair!" said Leslie. "Life had just gotten so beautiful! We worked so hard, we overcame so many problems . . . we were just beginning the good times."

I sighed. "Well, if we're dead, we're dead together. That part of our plans came true."

"Our lives are supposed to flash in front of us," she said. "Did your life flash in front of you?"

"Not yet," I said. "Yours?"

"No. And they say everything goes black. That's wrong, too!"

25

"How can so many books, how could *we* be so wrong?" I said. "Remember our out-of-body times at night? That's what dying ought to be, just like that except we'd go on, we wouldn't come back in the morning."

Ever had I believed that dying would make sense, it would be a rational creative chance for new understanding, a glad freedom from the limits of matter, an adventure beyond the walls of crude beliefs. Nothing had warned us that death is flying over an endless technicolor ocean.

At least we could land. There were no rocks, nor seaweed nor schools of fish. The water was smooth and clear, wind barely enough to ruffle the surface.

Leslie pointed the two bright paths to me. "It's like those two are friends," she said, "always together."

"Maybe they're runways," I said. "It feels best lining up on them. Let's touch down right where they join, OK? Ready to land?"

"I guess so," she said.

I looked out the side windows, double-checking our landing gear. "We have the left main *up*," I said, "nosewheel *up*, the right main is *up*, the wheels are *up* for a water landing, flaps are down. . . ."

We began the last turn and the sea tilted graceful slow-motion to meet us. We floated for a long moment, inches above the surface, reflections spangling our white hull.

The keel skimmed wavelets and the seaplane turned racing-boat, flying on a cloud of spray. The whisper of the engine faded into the rush of water as I pulled the throttle back and we slowed.

Then the water vanished, the airplane disappeared. Blurring around us were rooftops, streaks of red tiles and palm trees, the wall of some great windowed building dead ahead.

"LOOK OUT!"

The next second we were stopped inside that building, giddy but unscratched, standing together in a long hallway. I reached to my wife, held her.

"Are you all right?" we said together, breathless, the same second.

"Yes!" we said. "Not a scratch! Are you? Yes!"

There was no shattered glass in the window at the end of the hall, no hole in the wall through which we had rocketed. Not a person in sight, not a sound in the building.

I burst in frustration. "What in *hell* is going on?"

"Richie," she said quietly, eyes wide with wonder, "this place is familiar. We've been here before!"

I looked around. A many-doored hallway, brick-red carpet, elevator doors directly across from us, potted palms. The hall window overlooked sunny tile rooftops, low golden hills beyond, a hazy blue afternoon. "It's . . . it looks like a hotel. I don't remember any hotel. . . ."

Came a soft chime, a green arrowhead glowed above the elevator doors.

We watched as the doors rumbled open. Inside stood a

rangy angular man and a lovely woman dressed in faded work-shirt under a surplus Navy coat, bluejeans, a spice-color cap.

I heard my wife gasp at my side, felt her body tighten. From the elevator stepped the man and woman we had been sixteen years before, the two we were on the day we met.

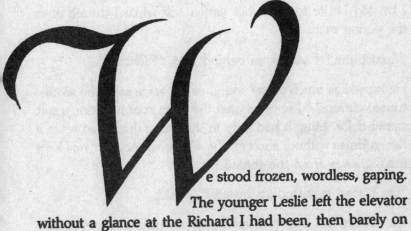

e stood frozen, wordless, gaping.

The younger Leslie left the elevator without a glance at the Richard I had been, then barely on the walk side of running, hurried toward her room.

Urgency overwhelmed amazement. We couldn't let them get away.

"Leslie! Wait!" my Leslie called.

The young woman stopped and turned, expecting a friend, but seemed not to recognize us. We must have been in shadow, or silhouette, the window behind us.

"Leslie," said my wife, walking toward her, "do you have a moment?"

The younger Richard, meanwhile, went past us toward his room. That the woman from the elevator had stumbled into friends was no business of his.

And that we don't know what's going on, I thought, doesn't keep us from being the ones in charge. It felt like a baby-chick roundup, these two going in opposite directions when we knew their destiny was to spend the rest of their lives together.

I trusted Leslie to catch her earlier self while I trotted after the young man.

"Excuse me," I said from behind him. "Richard?"

He turned as much at the sound of my voice as at the words, turned curiously. I remembered the sport coat he wore, a soft camel-color thing. It had a rip in the lining that I had sewn a dozen times without success; the silk or whatever it was kept tearing away from the thread.

"Do I need to introduce myself?" I said.

He looked at me, pleasant control turning to eyes like saucers.

"What . . . !"

"Look," I said, calm as I could, "we don't understand it either. We were flying and this weird thing hit us and. . . ."

"Are you . . . ?"

His voice trailed off and he stood there, staring. Of course it was a shock to him, but I felt strangely irritated at the guy. Who knew how much time we had together, minutes or less, hours or less, and he wants to waste it refusing to believe what should have been obvious?

"The answer is yes," I said. "I'm the man you're going to be a few years from now."

Shock turned to suspicion. "What was my mother's nickname for me?" he said, eyes narrowed.

I sighed and told him.

"What was the name of my dog, when I was a kid, and what kind of fruit did he eat?"

"Richard, come on!" I said. "Lady wasn't a he, she was a she. She ate apricots. You had a six-inch homebuilt Newtonian telescope with a chip on the mirror where you dropped a pair of pliers working on the spider with the tube up instead of down, there was a secret slat in the fence by your bedroom window, a slat with hinges you could slip through when you didn't want to use the gate. . . ."

"OK," he said, looking at me as if I were a magic act. "I suppose you could go on."

"Indefinitely. You can't ask a question about yourself that I can't answer, guy, and I've got sixteen years' more answers than you've got questions!"

He stared at me. A kid, I thought, not one gray hair. A little gray is going to look good on him.

"Would you like to waste whatever time we have chatting in the hall?" I said. Do you know that in the elevator there you've just met the woman you're . . . the most important person in your life and you *don't even know it*?"

"Her?" He looked down the hall, whispered to me. "But she's beautiful! How could she possibly. . . ."

"I don't understand it, but she finds you attractive. Take my word."

"OK, I believe it," he said. "I believe it!" He pulled a room key from his coat pocket. "Come on in."

Nothing made sense, but everything fit. This wasn't Los Angeles, this was Carmel, California, October 1972, third floor of the Holiday Inn. Before he turned the key, I knew the room would be scattered with radio-controlled model seagulls built for a film we had been shooting on the seashore. Some of the models flew lovely aerobatics, some of them tumbled end-over-end and crashed. I had dragged the wrecks to my room and glued them back together.

"I'll get Leslie," I said. "See if you can straighten the room up a bit, OK?"

"Leslie?"

"She's . . . well, there are two Leslies. One's the woman you just rode the elevator with, wishing you knew how to say hello. The stunning one is the same woman sixteen years later, my wife."

"I can't believe this!"

"Why don't you neaten the place," I said, "and we'll be right back."

I found Leslie in the hallway a few rooms away, her back to me, talking to her younger self. As I walked toward her, a maid emerged from the room nearby, headed toward the elevator, pushing a four-wheeled laundry cart. Without watching, she forced the heavy thing toward my wife.

"*Careful!*" I cried.

Too late. Leslie turned at my shout, but the cart hit her in the side, rolled on through her body as if she were air, the maid following, trampling through her, smiling hello to the younger woman as she did.

"Hey!" said the young Leslie, alarmed.

"Hey," replied the maid. "You have a good day!"

I ran to Leslie's side. "Are you OK?"

"Fine," she said. "I guess she didn't. . . ." She looked dismayed for a moment, turned back to the young woman. "Richard, I'd like you to meet Leslie Parrish. Leslie, this is my husband, Richard Bach."

I smiled at the formality of her introduction. "Hello," I said to the young woman. "Can you see me all right?"

She laughed up at me, eyes twinkling. "Are you supposed to be blurry?" No shock, no suspicion. The younger Leslie must have taken this for a dream and decided to enjoy it.

"Just checking," I said. "After what happened with the cart there, I'm not sure we're part of this world. I'll bet. . . ."

I reached to the wall, suspecting my hand would pass through the plaster. It did, wallpaper to the wrist. Young Leslie laughed, delighted.

"I think we're ghosts, here," I said.

33

So that's why we weren't dead on arrival, flying through the hotel wall, I thought.

How swiftly we adjust to incredible situations! Slip on a dockside, and at once we know we're over our heads in water: we move differently, breathe differently, in a half-second we're adapted, though we may not like the wet.

So with this. We were over our heads in our own past, startled we had fallen in, doing the best we knew in the strange place. And the best we knew was to get these two together, save them from losing the years we had lost before we knew we were soulmates.

It felt odd talking with the young woman, as though we were meeting again for the first time. How strange, I thought. She's Leslie, but I have no history with her!

"Maybe instead of standing here. . . ." I pointed down the hall. "Richard has invited us to his room. We might talk a little bit there, sort things out without laundry carts shuttling through us back and forth?"

She glanced in the hall mirror. "I wasn't planning on meeting anyone," she said. "I look a fright." She smoothed long strands of blonde hair under the edges of her cap.

I looked at my wife and we couldn't help but laugh.

"Good!" I said. "That was our last test for you. If Leslie Parrish ever faces a mirror and says she looks OK, she's not the real Leslie Parrish!"

I led the way to Richard's door, knocked before I thought. My knuckles disappeared in the wood without a sound, of course.

"I guess you'd better knock," I said to young Leslie.

She did, a gay little tapping rhythm, showing off that *her* touch made not only sound but music.

The door opened at once, Richard holding a forty-inch balsa-wood seagull by one wingtip.

"Hi," I said. "Richard, I'd like you to meet Leslie Parrish, your future wife. Leslie, this is Richard Bach, your husband-to-be."

He leaned the seagull against the wall, shook hands formally with the young woman, his face a curious mixture of eagerness and dread as he looked at her.

The bemused twinkle never left her eyes as she looked up at him, shaking his hand as gravely as she could. "I'm very happy to meet you," she said.

"And Richard, this is my wife, Leslie Parrish-Bach."

"Hello," he nodded.

He stood still a long moment, looking from one Leslie to the other to me, as if a band of Halloween tricksters had come to his door.

"Come on in," he said at last. "The place is a mess. . . ."

He wasn't kidding. If he'd cleaned it, it didn't show. Wooden birds, radio control modules, batteries, sheets of balsa-wood, junk on windowsills, all smelling of model-airplane paint.

He had set out four glasses of water on the coffee table, three little bags of corn chips, a can of peanuts. If our hands go through the walls, I thought, we probably won't be too lucky with the corn chips.

"To put your mind at ease, Miss Parrish," he began, "I was married once, but never will be again. I don't quite understand who these people are, but I assure you that I have zero intention of making any approach of any kind. . . ."

"Oh, God," said my wife, sotto voce, looking to the ceiling, "the anti-marriage speech."

"Wookie, please," I whispered. "He's a nice fellow, he's just frightened. Let's not. . . ."

"Wookie?" said the young Leslie.

"Excuse me," I said. "Nickname from a movie we saw a long time . . . a long time from now." I began to sense that this could be a difficult talk ahead.

"First things first," said my wife, organizing the incredible. "Richard and I don't know how we got here, we don't know how long we're going to stay, we don't know where we're going. The only thing we know is you, we know your past and your future, at least the next sixteen years of it."

"You two are going to fall in love," I said. "You're already in love, you just don't know that each of you is the person the other would love if you knew each other. Right now you think there isn't anyone in the world who can understand you, or love you. But there is, and here you are!"

The younger Leslie sat on the floor, leaned against the bed, suppressed a smile. She drew her knees to her chin. "Do we have anything to do with this love of ours, or is it unstoppable destiny?"

"Good question," said Leslie. "Let us tell you what we remember, what happened to us." She paused, puzzled at what she was about to say. "Then you have to do what you think is right for you."

What we remember, I thought. I remember this place, I remember seeing Leslie in the elevator, but not getting to know her for years. I remembered no meetings here with future Leslies, nor future Richards telling me to neaten my room.

The young Richard sat on a desk chair, looked at the young Leslie. Her physical beauty was for him just this side of the threshold of pain. He was shy around beautiful women, never guessed she was just as shy as he.

"When we met, appearances blocked us, other people blocked us from even trying to know each other," said my Leslie.

"We made mistakes apart that we never would have made together," I said. "But now that you know . . . don't you see? You don't have to make those mistakes!"

"By the time we met again years later," Leslie went on, "all we could do was pick up the pieces and hope we could still build the enchanted life we could have had years before. If we'd met sooner we wouldn't have had to go through all that *recovering*. Of course, we *did* meet sooner, we met in the elevator the same as you did. We just weren't brave enough or smart enough. . . ." She shook her head. "We didn't have whatever it took to know who we could be to each other."

"So we think you're crazy not to fall into each other's arms right now," I went on, "to thank God you've met, and set about changing your lives to be together."

Our younger selves glanced at one another, looked away quickly.

"We wasted so much time when we were you," I said, "we passed up so many chances to steer away from disasters and fly!"

"Disasters?" said Richard.

"Disasters," I told him. "You're in the middle of several right now. You just don't know it yet."

"You made it through," he said. "Do you think you're the only one who can solve problems? You have all the answers?"

Why was he so defensive? I paced by the edge of the table, looking down at him. "We have some answers, but the important thing for you is to know that *she's* got most of 'em, and you've got answers for her, too. Together, there's nothing can stop you!"

"Can stop us from what?" said young Leslie, caught by the intensity of my feelings, suspecting at last that this might not be a dream.

"From living your highest love," said my wife, "reaching a life together so wonderful you can't imagine it apart!"

How could these two resist the once-in-never gift we offered them? How often do we talk with the people we're going to become, the ones who know every mistake we're going to make? They had the chance that everybody wishes for but no one gets.

My wife sat on the floor, next to Leslie, the older of twins. "In the privacy of this room, just us, we need to tell you: for all your mistakes, each of you is an extraordinary person. You've held to your sense of right, your inner ethics, even when it's been hard or dangerous or when people called you strange. That strangeness sets you apart. It makes you lonely. It also makes you perfect for each other."

The two listened so carefully I couldn't read their faces. "Is she right?" I asked them. "Tell us to get lost if this is nonsense. If it's not true, we can run along. We have our own little problem to work out. . . ."

"No!" they said together.

"One thing you've told us," said the young Leslie, "we'll live another sixteen years! No wars, no end of the world. But . . . maybe that's a question. Did *we* survive this time, or did you?"

"Do you think we know what's going on?" I said. "Wrong! We don't even know if we're dead or alive! All we know is somehow it's possible, without all the gears falling out of the universe, for us from your future to meet you from our past."

"We want something from you," said Leslie.

Her younger self looked up, the same beautiful eyes. "What's that?"

"We're the ones who come after you, we're the ones who pay for your mistakes, who profit from your striving. We're the ones proud of your best choices and sad for your worst.

39

We're the closest friends you'll have besides each other. Whatever happens, don't forget us, don't sell us out!"

"You know what we've learned?" I said. "Short-term comfort for long-term trouble is not the trade you're looking for. The easy way is not the easy way!" I turned to the younger me. "Do you know how many offers like that are going to come to you between your time and ours?"

"Lots?"

I nodded. "Lots."

"How do we keep from wrong turns?" he asked. "I have a feeling I've already taken the easy way a couple of times."

"To be expected," I said. "Wrong turns are as important as right turns. More important, sometimes."

"They're not very comfortable," he said.

"No, but they're. . . ."

"Are you the only future we have?" The young Leslie spoke suddenly, cutting me off in the importance of her question, and for no reason I felt a bolt of fear when she asked.

"Are you our only past?" answered my wife.

"Of course. . . ." said Richard.

"Not!" I stared at him, thunderstruck. "Of course not! That's why we don't remember any us-from-the-future at the Carmel Holiday Inn! We don't remember because it didn't happen to us, it happened to *you!*"

Implications fired like lasers through everyone in the room. Here we perched, giving these two the best we knew, but could they be just one of our pasts, one of the paths that led to who we are? For a moment we meant safety to them, we confirmed their survival. But could it be that we weren't their inevitable future waiting, could there be other choices for them, different turns than we had taken?

"It doesn't matter whether we're your future or not," said my wife. "Don't turn your backs on the love. . . ."

She stopped midsentence, looked at me startled. The room was trembling, a low rumble through the building.

"Earthquake?" I said.

"No. There's no earthquake," said the younger Leslie. "I don't feel a thing. Richard?"

He shook his head. "Nothing."

For us the whole room was shaking now, slow frequencies going faster each second.

My wife stood suddenly, frightened. Having survived two major earthquakes, she was not eager for number three. I reached for her hand. "The mortals in the room don't feel any earthquake, wookie, and we ghosts don't mind falling plaster. . . ."

And then the place was shuddering like pale blue in a paintshaker, the walls blurring, the roar louder than ever, the younger us mystified by what was happening to Leslie and me. The only solid was my wife at my side, holding on, calling out to those two.

"*Stay*," she cried, "*together!*"

In a moment the hotel room shook itself out of sight, engulfed in engine-roar and pouring water. Spray flew back, wind-blasted from the glass, and there we were in the cabin of our flying-boat once more, engine instruments trembling on their redlines, shallow sea thudding beneath us, the Sea-bird already light on her hull, ready to fly.

Leslie shrieked with relief and patted the airplane's glareshield lovingly. "*Growly!* It's so good to see you!"

I eased the control wheel toward me and in a few seconds our little ship broke free of the water, trailing a veil of spray, those intricate lines of the seafloor falling away beneath us. How safe it felt to be in the air again!

"It was Growly's takeoff!" I said. "Growly pulled us out of Carmel! But what do you suppose pushed the throttle forward? What got the takeoff started?"

The answer came before Leslie could speak, a voice from behind us.

"I did."

We turned the same instant, dumb surprise. All of a sudden, three hundred feet in the air over a world we didn't know, we had a passenger on board.

t once my hand cocked to drive the control wheel forward, pin the intruder to the overhead.

"Don't be frightened!" she said. "I'm friendly!" She laughed. "Of all people, don't be scared of *me*!"

My hand relaxed a little.

"Who . . . ?" said Leslie, staring at the woman.

Our passenger, dressed in jeans and plaid blouse, had smooth dark skin, hair to her shoulders the color of brushed India, eyes black as midnight.

"My name is Pye," she said, "and I am to you as you are to

those you left in Carmel." She shrugged, correcting herself. "Times several thousand."

I brought the engine back to low cruise, the noise fell away. "How did you . . . ?" I said. "What are you doing here?"

"I thought you might feel concerned," she said. "I came to help."

"What do you mean, times several thousand?" said Leslie. "Are you me from the future?"

She nodded, leaning forward to speak. "I'm you both. Not from the future, but from. . . ." She hummed a curious coupled note. ". . . an alternate now."

I yearned to know how she could be us both, what's an alternate now, but most of all I wanted to know what was happening.

"Where are we?" I asked. "Do you know what killed us?"

She smiled, shook her head. "Killed you? What makes you think you're dead?"

"I don't know," I said. "We were letting down into Los Angeles and all of a sudden there was a big hum and the city disappeared, is all. What was civilization vaporizes in half a second and we're alone over some ocean that doesn't exist on the planet earth and when we land we're ghosts looking at our own past, the people we were when we met, and no one can see us but them, and people push laundry carts through us and our arms go through the walls. . . ." I shrugged helplessly. "Aside from that, I can't imagine why we'd think we're dead."

She laughed. "Well, you're not dead."

My wife and I looked at each other, felt a wave of relief.

"Then where are we?" asked Leslie. "What happened to us?"

"This is not a place as much as it is a point of perspective," said Pye. "And what happened probably has to do with electronics." She looked at our instrument panel, frowned. "You've got very-high-frequency transmitters here. Loran receiver, the transponder, radar pulses. It could have been an interaction. Cosmic rays. . . ." She scanned the instruments, paused. "Was there a big golden flash?"

"Yes!"

"Interesting," she said with a little smile. "Chances of this happening are one in trillions!" She was totally engaging, warm family. "You shouldn't count on taking this trip too often."

"Is it one in trillions to get back?" I asked. "We have a meeting in Los Angeles tomorrow. Can we get there in time?"

"Time?" She turned to Leslie. "Are you hungry?"

"No."

Then to me. "Thirsty?"

"No."

"Why do you suppose not?"

"Excitement," I said. "Stress."

"Fear!" said Leslie.

"Are you afraid?" Pye asked.

Leslie thought for a moment, smiled at her. "Not anymore."

I couldn't say the same. Change is not my favorite sport.

She turned to me. "How much fuel are you using?"

The gage was still frozen.

"None!" I said, suddenly understanding. "Growly's using no fuel, we're using no fuel because fuel and hunger and thirst are time-related and there's no time here!"

Pye nodded.

"Speed is time-related," said Leslie, "but we're moving."

"Are you?" Pye raised her dark eyebrows in question, turned to me.

"Don't look at me," I said. "We're moving only in belief? We're moving only in. . . ."

Pye gave an encouraging you're-getting-warm signal, as though we were playing charades, or Fifteen Questions.

". . . consciousness?"

She touched the tip of her nose, flashed a bright smile. "Exactly! Time is your name for the motion of consciousness. Every possible event that can happen in space and time happens *now*, at once, simultaneous. There is no past, there is no future, only *now*, though we have to use a time-based language so we can talk.

"It's like. . . ." She looked to the ceiling for a simile. "It's like arithmetic. As soon as you know the system, you know that every problem in numbers is already answered. The principle of arithmetic already knows the cube root of six, but it may take us what we call time, a few seconds, to find out what the answer has always been."

The cube root of 8 is 2, I thought, the cube root of 1 is 1. Cube root of 6? Somewhere between 1 and 2, on the high side — 1.8? And sure enough, while I calculated, I knew that the answer had been waiting since before I had asked the question.

"Every event?" said Leslie. "Every possible thing that can happen has *already happened*? There is no future?"

"Nor past," said Pye, "nor time."

Leslie, ever practical, was exasperated. "Then why do we live through all these experiences in this . . . this make-believe time if everything's already done? *Why bother?*"

"The point is not that it's done, but that we have infinite choice," said Pye. "Our choices lead us to our experiences, and with experience we realize that we are not the little creatures we seem to be. We're interdimensional expressions of life, mirrors of spirit."

"Where does all this happen?" I said. "Is there some big warehouse in the sky, with shelves of all these possible events to choose from?"

"Not a warehouse. Not a place, though you may perceive it as a place," she said. "Where do you think it might be?"

I shook my head, turned to Leslie. She shook her head, too.

Pye asked again, dramatically. "Where?" Watching our eyes, she raised her hand, pointed downward.

We looked. Below us, underwater, turned those endless paths on the ocean floor.

"The pattern?" said Leslie. "Under the water? Oh! Our choices! The pattern represents the paths we took, the turns we made! And every possible other turn we could have made, that we *have* made in. . . ."

". . . parallel lifetimes?" I asked, watching pieces fall together. "Alternate lifetimes!"

The pattern sprawled majestically below us; we goggled down in wonder.

"We fly up high," I said, trembling with insight, "and we have perspective! We see every choice and fork and crossroad. But the lower we fly, the more we lose perspective. And when we land, our perspective on all the other choices is gone! We focus on detail: daily hourly minute-ly detail, alternate lifetimes forgotten!"

"What a pretty metaphor you've built to explore who you are," said Pye, "a pattern under endless water. You do have to fly your seaplane here and there to visit your alternate selves, but it's a creative tool and it works."

"This sea underneath us, then," I said, "it isn't a sea, is it? The pattern isn't really there."

"Nothing in spacetime is really there," she said. "The pattern is a visual aid you've built, it's your way of understanding simultaneous lifetimes. It's a metaphor of flight because you love flying. When you land, your seaplane floats above the pattern, and you're observers, you're ghosts in your alternate worlds. You can learn from your other aspects without taking their surroundings for real. When you've learned what you need to learn, you remember your seaplane, push the throttle forward and you're swept into the air, back with your grand perspective."

"We designed this . . . pattern?" asked Leslie.

"There are as many metaphors for lives in spacetime as there are disciplines that fascinate you," said Pye. "If you loved photography, your metaphor could have turned on levels of focus. Focus makes one point sharp and everything else a blur. We focus on one lifetime and we think that's all there is. But all those other aspects, the misty ones we take for dreams and wishes and might-have-beens, they're as real as any other. We choose our focus."

"Is this why we're fascinated with physics," I asked, "with quantum mechanics, with timelessness? None of it's possible, but all of it's true? No past lives, no future lives, zoom down to one point, believe it's moving and we've invented time? Get involved and we think it's the only life there is? Is that right, Pye?"

"Close enough," she said.

"Then we can fly ahead," said Leslie, "beyond the place where we left young Richard and Leslie in Carmel, we can land ahead of them and find out whether they stayed together. We can see if they saved those years we lost!"

"You already know," said our otherworld guide.

"We don't!" I said. "We were pulled away. . . ."

Pye smiled. "They have choices, too. One aspect of them is frightened and runs from a future too full of commitment. Another becomes friends but never lovers, another becomes lovers but never friends, another marries and divorces, another decides to see each other as soulmates, marries and loves forever."

"So we're like tourists here!" I said. "We don't build the landscape, we just choose which part of it we want to see!"

"That's a nice way of looking at it," said Pye.

"OK," I said, "let's pretend we fly to a slice of the pattern where we land and keep our mother from meeting our father. If they don't meet, how could we have been born?"

"No, Richie," said Leslie, "that wouldn't stop us from being born. We were born in the part of the pattern where they *did* meet and nothing can change that!"

"Nothing's predetermined?" I asked. "There's no destiny?"

"Of course there's destiny," said Pye, "but destiny doesn't push you where you don't want to go. You're the ones who choose. Destiny's up to you."

"We'd choose to go home, Pye," I said. "How do we get back?"

She smiled. "Going home is easy as jumping off a log. Your pattern is a psychic one, but the way back is spiritual. Guide yourselves by love. . . ." She stopped suddenly. "Forgive the lecture. Would you like to go now?"

"Please."

"No!" said Leslie. She talked to Pye, but reached for my

hand, her way of saying hear me out. "If I understand you, the people we were, the ones flying to Los Angeles, are stopped in time. We can go back to them whenever we choose."

"Sure we can," I said, "but the next instant comes our cosmic-ray burst and here we are again!"

"No," said Pye. "The instant you return, a million variables change. Any one will keep it from happening again. Would you like to go?"

"No," said Leslie again. "I want to learn from this, Richie, I want to understand! If we only have one chance in trillions and this is it, we have to stay!"

"Pye," I said, "if we stay, can we get hurt, off in some other time, can we get hurt even though we're ghosts?"

"You can choose that if you wish," she said.

"Choose it?" It sounded ominous to me. I take my adventures gently. Flying into the utterly unknown is not adventure, it's insanity. Could we get caught in this pattern of belief and lose the world we had? What if we got separated and never found each other again? Beliefs can be ferocious traps. I turned to my wife, a little nervous. "I think we'd better get back, sweetie."

"Oh, Richie, do you really want to give up this chance? Isn't this what you've always read about, your life-long fascination, simultaneous lifetimes, alternate futures? Think of what we'd learn! Isn't it worth a little danger?"

I sighed. Leslie's past is all brave choices in search of truth

51

and principle. Of course she'd choose to stay. Now she appealed to the explorer at the edge of my mind.

"OK, little darling," I said at last.

The air was heavy with underestimated risk. I felt like a student pilot off to learn slow rolls without a safety belt.

"Pye, how many aspects of us are there, anyway?" I asked.

She laughed, looked out the window to the pattern below. "How many can you imagine? There is no counting."

"That whole pattern is *us?*" said Leslie, dumbfounded. "As far as we see, as far as we fly, the pattern is *our choices?*"

She nodded.

We haven't started, I thought, and it's already beyond believing. "What about everybody else, Pye? How many lives can there be in one universe?"

She looked at me puzzled, as if she didn't understand my question. "How many lives in the universe, Richard?" she asked. "One."

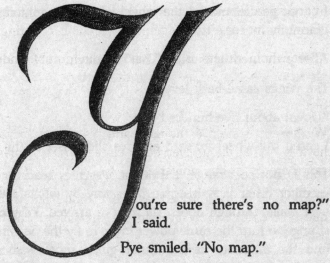

ou're sure there's no map?" I said.

Pye smiled. "No map."

So much of flying is chart-reading, I thought. We put a dot on our paper: this is where we are. Another dot: this is where we want to go. Between them, a torrent of angles and bearings and distances, headings and times. Now, in an endless country we'd never seen, the compass didn't work and we had no map.

"Intuition is your guide here," said Pye. "One level of you knows everything there is to know. Find that level, ask for guidance, and trust you'll be led wherever you most need to go. Try it."

Leslie closed her eyes at once, relaxed beside me as we flew, doing her best to follow instructions. The pattern unfurled serene beneath us, our strange passenger sat unspeaking, and my wife was quiet so long she could have been asleep.

"Turn right," said Leslie softly, at last. She didn't tell me steep right or gentle right, she didn't give me degrees to turn.

I chose gentle, moved the wheel and the amphibian tilted gracefully into the turn.

After a moment she said, "That's enough. . . ."

The wings came back level.

"Down about five hundred feet."

I eased the wheel forward and we slid closer to the waves.

This is not so strange, I thought. Psychics reaching to remember other lives imagine their way by what feels right, over walls, through doors, till they've arrived. Why count it strange to turn the same power loose to fly the Seabird, let it find the alternate us our inner guide most wishes we'd meet? And if it doesn't work, what have we lost?

"Turn right again," said Leslie. Then, almost at once, "Straight. And down another five hundred feet."

"That'll put us right above the water," I said.

She nodded, eyes still closed. "Get ready to land."

There had been no change in the design below: infinite complexity as far as we could see. Rainbow swirls and intersections and parallels gave way to shifts and sweeps and fans, pastels to silver. Sparkling over it all, the crystal sea of this strange world.

I turned to Pye, but in answer she looked a wordless wait-and-see.

"Right turn," Leslie said. "We're almost there. Tiny bit to the left. . . . Now power off, land!"

I cut the throttle and the keel touched the waves at once. Leslie opened her eyes at the sound of the water, watched as eagerly as I while the world dissolved in spray. The Seabird disappeared, and Pye with it. Leslie and I plummeted together through a golden dusk past trees on a river-bank, then the side of an old stone house.

We stopped in the living room, dim and gray, low ceilings, a boarded-up fireplace in one corner, wavy scarred wooden floors, an orange-crate for a table, battered upright piano against one wall. Even the light in the room was gray.

On an old chair in front of the piano sat a thin young woman. Her hair was long and blonde, her clothes threadbare. The music rack in front of her overflowed with heavy books of Brahms, Bach, Schumann. She was playing a Beethoven sonata from memory, glorious sound through that wreck of an instrument.

Leslie watched, awestruck. "This is my house," she whispered, "the house in Upper Black Eddy! Richie, that's me!"

I stared. My wife had told me there had not been much to eat when she was growing up, but this girl verged on starvation. No wonder Leslie rarely looked back. If my past had been that bleak I wouldn't look back, either.

The girl didn't notice us, played on as if she were in heaven.

At the doorway to the kitchen a woman appeared, listened quietly to the music, an envelope open in her hand. She was small and pretty, but as thin and threadbare as the girl.

"Mom!" Leslie cried, her voice breaking.

The woman didn't see us, didn't answer. She waited quietly until the music stopped.

"Honey, that's beautiful," she said to the girl's back, shaking her head sadly. "It really is, and I'm proud of you. But there's no future in it!"

"Momma, please. . . ." said the girl.

"You have to be realistic," her mother went on. "Pianists are a dime a dozen. You remember what the priest told you, his sister never could make a living from the piano. And that was after years and years of schooling!"

"Oh, Mom!" The girl threw her arms up in exasperation. "Not the priest's sister again! Can't you tell that the priest's sister is a terrible pianist? She can't make a living because she's *awful!*"

Her mother ignored that. "Do you know how much school you'll have to have? Do you know what school costs?"

The girl set her jaw, looked straight ahead at her music, nodded grimly. "I know exactly how much. I have three jobs now, Mother, I'll get the money."

The woman sighed. "Don't be cross with me, sweetheart. I'm only trying to help. I don't want you to pass up these wonderful chances the way I did and then regret it all your life. I sent your picture to New York because I knew it could be your way out. What matters is, you've won! They've *accepted* you!"

She put the envelope on the music rack. "At least look at it. You have a chance to be a model with one of the biggest agencies in New York City and stop this endless struggle . . . waitress jobs and cleaning houses and working yourself to death!"

"I'm not working myself *to death!*"

"Look at you! You're thin as a rail. You think you can keep this up, running back and forth to Philadelphia because you can't afford to stay more than one night, crushing college into two days a week? You can't. You're only seventeen and you're exhausted! Why won't you listen to reason?"

The girl sat rigid, silent. Her mother watched, shook her head in bewilderment. "Every girl would love to be a model and you want to turn it down! Honey, *listen.* Go and try it for a year or so and save as much as you can and *then* go on with your music if you still want to."

The girl reached for the envelope, handed it back over her shoulder without looking. "I don't want to go New York," she said, trying to control her anger. "I don't care if I won. I don't want to be a model. And I don't mind struggling if that's what it takes to do what I love."

Her mother snatched the letter, patience gone. "Is that piano the only thing you can think of?"

"*Yes!*"

The girl drowned further talk with her hands, filling the

room with the sounds from the pages in front of her, her fingers butterflies one minute, steel the next. How can arms that thin, I thought, have so much power?

Her mother watched for a moment, took the letter out of the envelope, set it open on the orange crate and walked out the back door. The girl played on.

I knew from what Leslie had told me that tomorrow would be her recital in Philadelphia. She would get up at four the next morning to start a journey of sixty-five miles, six hours by foot and bus and trolley. She'd have classes all day, play in recital at night. Then she would sleep in the bus station till morning classes, saving her room rent to buy music.

Leslie left me suddenly and walked to stand beside the girl, who ignored her.

I looked fascinated at the music and thought how strange! It was *new*. Those are the same books, their pages now yellow, that grace our piano still.

At last the girl turned to Leslie — a pale, lovely face with features like her mother's, blue eyes flashing resentment.

"If you're from the modeling agency," she said on the edge of anger, "the answer is no. Thank you, but no."

Leslie shook her head. "I'm not from Conover," she said.

The girl looked at her for a long moment, then rose to her feet, her mouth open in astonishment. "You're. . . . You look like me!" she gasped. "You *are* me! Aren't you?"

My wife nodded.

The girl stared. "But you're grown up!"

She stood surrounded by her poverty and her dreams and looked into her future, gazed in silence at my wife, and at last her stony wall of determination broke.

She sank back to her chair, covered her face with her hands. "Help me," she cried, "please help me!"

y wife knelt beside the child she had been, looking up to her. "It's all right," she soothed. "It's going to be all right. You're such a lucky girl! You really are!"

The girl sat up, looked at her unbelieving, brushed tears with her hands.

"Lucky? You call this luck?" She almost laughed with hope through the tearstreaks.

"Luck, gift, privilege. You've found what you love! So few people find that at your age. Some *never* do. You already know."

"Music."

My wife nodded, stood. "You have such gifts: you're bright and talented, you love your music, and you have as much determination as anyone alive. Nothing can stop you!"

"Why do I have to be so *poor*? If only. . . . This piano is . . . listen!" She struck the keyboard four times, eight notes in lightning octaves. Even I could tell there were strings broken inside. "G-sharp and D don't play at all and we can't afford to tune. . . ." She pounded her fist on the yellow keys. "*Why?*"

"So you can prove that determination and love and hard work can lift you from poverty and despair. And maybe someday you'll meet some other kid who lives in poverty. And when she says, 'Oh, everything's easy for you because you're a famous pianist, you're rich, but I don't have enough to eat, I have this piece of junk to practice on. . . .' you can pass on a bit of experience, help *her* to hang on."

The girl thought about it. "I'm whining," she said, "and I don't know why. I *hate* whining!"

"It's OK to complain to me," said Leslie.

"Am *I* going to hang on? To succeed?" asked the girl.

"The choices are yours, more than you suspect." Leslie glanced at me. "If you never let go of what matters to you, if it matters so much that you're willing to struggle this hard to have it, I promise you'll have a very successful life. A hard life, because excellence is not easy, but a good life."

"Could I have an easy, bad life?"

"That's a choice, too."

Mischief glittered. "How about an easy, happy life?"

They both laughed. "Possible," Leslie said. "But you wouldn't choose an easy life, would you?"

The young girl looked at her approvingly. "I want to do just what you did!"

"No," said Leslie with a sad smile. "You follow your own course, go your own way."

"Are you happy?"

"Yes!"

"Then I want to do what you did."

She studied the girl for a moment, decided to confide the worst. "I'm not sure that you do. I've had times that were so terrible I didn't want to live at all. Lots of times. Times I tried to end it. . . ."

The girl caught her breath. "Me, too!"

"I know," said Leslie. "I know how hard it is for you to go on."

"But you did it. How?"

Leslie turned away, ashamed to tell her. "I took the job with Conover. I gave up the piano."

The girl stood, numb, unable to believe. "How *could* you? What . . . what about love and determination?"

Leslie turned back. "I know how you're getting by in Philadelphia—sleeping in the bus station, spending your room rent and food money to buy music. Mom would faint if she knew. You're on the edge of disaster all the time."

The girl nodded.

"I was the same," said Leslie. "Then one of my jobs fell through and I couldn't hang on, even starving. I was desperate, I was furious, but I had to face it, Mom was right.

"I promised myself I'd go to New York for just one year, work night and day, save every cent and earn enough to go straight for my master's degree. . . ." The sentence ended in wistful memory.

"But you didn't earn *any*thing?"

"No . . . I earned a lot. Success hit me like a cloudburst at first: modeling, then television. In a year I was in Hollywood under contract to Twentieth Century-Fox, making movies. But it was success in a business I didn't love. I never felt good enough or pretty enough; I never felt I belonged there.

"I could help the family, so I couldn't justify quitting and going back to music. But I didn't choose to stay in films either, I just *stayed*—a default decision."

She paused a moment, thinking back.

"My heart wasn't in it, you see, so I could only allow myself a limited amount of success. Every time it threatened to go beyond that, I'd turn down a great part or run away or get sick—I'd do something to wreck it. There was never a clear choice to really succeed."

It was quiet for a moment, the two considering what she said.

"But how could I complain about all the good things that were happening to me? I couldn't tell anyone. I felt alone. I was unhappy for years." Leslie sighed. "So. When I gave up music I got as much success as I could tolerate. I got adventure, challenge, excitement, tremendous learning. . . ."

"It doesn't sound all bad. . . ." the young girl said.

My wife nodded. "I know. That's why it was so hard to understand, so hard to walk away. But years later I realized that when I gave up music I gave up my chance for a peaceful, joyful life doing what I really loved. Gave it up for a long time, at least."

I listened, surprised. Only now was I seeing what might have been, what my wife had put aside when she leaped from music to the ice of her Hollywood career.

The girl looked totally confused. "Well, that was true for you, but will it be true for me? What should *I* do?"

"You're the only one in the world who can answer that question. Find out what you really want to do and do it. Don't spend twenty years living your life by default when you can decide right now to go in the direction of your love. *What do you really want?*"

She knew at once. "I want to learn. I want to be excellent at what I do," she said. "I want to give something special to the world!"

"You will. What else?"

"I want to be happy. I don't want to be poor."

"Yes. What else?"

She warmed to the game. "I want to believe there's some reason for living that makes sense, some principle to help me through hard times and good times, too. It's not religion because I've tried it, I really have, and instead of answers I get 'Have Faith My Child.'"

Leslie frowned, remembering.

The young woman went on, suddenly shy. "I want to believe there's someone else in the world who's just as alone as I am. I want to believe we're going to find each other and . . . and love each other, and never be alone again!"

"Listen," said my wife. "Everything you've said, everything you want to believe is *already true.* You may not find some of it for a little while, and some of it may take longer than that, but that doesn't keep it from being true this minute!"

"Even the someone to love? Is there really someone for me? Is he true too?"

"His name is Richard. Want to meet him?"

"Meet him *now?*" she said, her eyes filled with wonder.

My wife held out her hand to me. I walked from behind the girl, glad that this aspect of one so dear would want to meet me.

She looked up at me speechless.

"Hi," I said, a little awestruck myself. How strange to look into that face, so different from the woman I loved, so much the same!

"You seem too . . . so . . . grown-up for me." She'd finally found a tactful way of saying *old.*

"By the time you meet me, you'll love older men," I said.

"I do *not* love older men!" said my wife, putting her arm around my waist. "I love *this* older man. . . ."

The girl watched us. "Is it OK to ask . . . are you really happy together?" She said it as if she found it hard to believe.

"Happier than you can imagine," I said.

"When do I meet you? Where? At the Conservatory?"

Should I tell her the truth? That it would take her another twenty-five years, a failed marriage, other men? That it would be a lifetime-and-a-half from where she stood by her battered piano before we'd meet?

I looked the question to my wife.

"It'll be quite some time," she said gently.

"Oh."

It'll be quite some time must have made her feel more alone than ever.

She turned to me. "And what did you decide to be?" she asked. "Are you a pianist, too?"

"No," I said. "I fly airplanes. . . ."

She glanced at Leslie, disappointed.

". . . but I'm learning to play the flute."

I could tell she was not impressed with amateur flute players. She let it go, determined to find my brighter side, leaned toward me earnestly. "What can you teach me," she said, "what do you *know*?"

"I know we're all in school," I said. "And we have some required courses: Survival, Nourishment and Shelter," I said pointedly. She smiled a guilty smile, knowing I'd heard her money-saving secrets. "You know what else I know?"

"What?"

"Arguments won't, facts won't, debates won't change your mind. Your problems are easy for us to solve; every problem is easy after you've already found the answer. But even your own future self, materialized out of empty air in front of you, telling you word for word what you'll find in the next thirty-five years, is not going to change your mind. The only thing that will ever change it is your own personal individual insight!"

"You want me to learn that from you?" She laughed. "My whole family thinks I'm stubborn and strange. They'd hate to hear you encourage me."

"Why do you think we came to see you?" asked Leslie.

"Because you think I'll kill myself?" asked the girl. "Because you wish some future self would have come to *you* at my age and said don't worry, you'll survive! Isn't that right?"

Leslie nodded.

"I promise to survive," the girl said. "Better than that, I promise you'll be glad I lived, I promise you'll be proud of me!"

"I am proud of you!" said Leslie. "We're both proud of you. My life was in your hands, and you didn't let me die, you didn't give up when everything around you was despair. Maybe we didn't come back to save you, maybe we came back to thank you for opening the way, for making it possible for Richard and me to find each other and be so happy. Maybe we came back to tell you that we love you."

The world began to tremble around us, the drab scene blurred, we were being pulled away.

The girl knew we were leaving, brushed tears from her eyes. "Will I see you again?"

"We hope so. . . ." said Leslie through tears of her own.

"Thank you for coming!" she called after us. "Thank you!"

We must have disappeared to her, for through the blur we could see her sag against the piano, head down for a moment. Then she sat on the old chair and her fingers began to move on the keys.

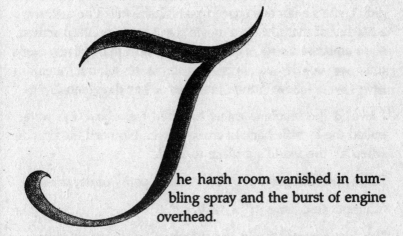he harsh room vanished in tumbling spray and the burst of engine overhead.

Pye took her hand from the throttle, settled into the back seat and watched us, warm support.

"She had such a hard life!" said Leslie, drying her tears. "She was so alone! Is it fair that we should get the rewards of her courage and her hard work?"

"Remember she chose that life," said Pye. "She chose the rewards, too."

"Rewards?" Leslie asked.

"Isn't she part of you right now?"

Of course, I thought. Her delight in her music, her one-track stubborn mind, even her body, smoothed and finished by years of decisions, didn't she sit with us now, as we flew?

"I guess so," said Leslie. "I just wonder what happened to her. . . ."

"Everything happened to her," said Pye. "She stayed with her music and she didn't, she went to New York and she didn't, she's a famous concert pianist, she killed herself, she's a teacher of math, she's a movie star, she's a political activist, she's ambassador to Argentina. Every turn in our lives, every time we decide, we become parents to all our alternate selves who follow. You're just one of her daughters."

I leveled the seaplane a few hundred feet above the water, pulled the throttle back to cruise power. No need for altitude when all the world's a place to land.

Below, the designs swept by, endless paths underwater.

"Complicated, isn't it?" I said.

"It's like tapestry," said Pye. "Thread by thread, it's simple. Try weaving by the yard and it gets a little tangled."

"Do you miss your early selves?" I asked our guide. "Do you miss us?"

She smiled. "How can I miss you when we're never apart? I don't live in spacetime. I'm always with you."

"But Pye," I said, "you have a body. It may not be quite the same as ours, but it does have a certain size, a certain look. . . ."

"No. I don't have a body. You perceive my presence, and you choose to perceive it as a body. There's a wide spectrum of other perceptions that you could have chosen, all of them useful, none of them true."

Leslie turned to look at her. "What higher perception could we have chosen?"

I turned, too, and saw a blue-white star of pure light, a carbon arc in the cabin. The world went incandescent.

We jerked away. I clamped my eyes shut, yet that blaze of light still roared. Then the fire was gone, Pye touched our shoulders, and we could see again.

"I'm sorry," she said, "how thoughtless of me! You can't see me as I am, you can't touch me as I am. We can't speak in words and say the whole truth because language can't describe. . . . For me to say *I* and not mean *you-us-all-spirit-One* is to speak lies, but not to speak in words is to miss this chance to talk. Better well-intentioned lies than silence, or no talking at all. . . ."

My eyes were still afire with the light. "My God, Pye, when do we learn to do *that?*"

She laughed. "You already are that. What you've had to learn in spacetime is to keep your lights out!"

I was more puzzled than ever, and nervous over needing this person. However kind she seemed to be, she was in control of our lives. "Pye, when we want to come back from those alternate selves where we land, how can *we* move the plane to take us away?"

"You don't need the seaplane at all. Or the pattern. You

shape them with your imagination and do with them what you will. And as you imagine, so your world seems to be."

"I imagine lifting my hand to the throttle? How can I move my hand to the throttle when I'm in some other world? How can I be in two places at once? If you hadn't gotten us out of there, we'd have been trapped in 1952!"

"You're not two places at once, you're everywhere at once. And you rule your worlds, they do not rule you. Would you like to try again?"

Leslie touched my knee, took the controls. "Try it, sweetie," she said. "Tell me where to fly."

I settled deep in the seat, closed my eyes. "Straight ahead," I said, feeling foolish. I could as easily have said straight up.

The engine lulled us along for a while. Then, though I saw nothing, there was a sudden sense of purpose in the dark.

"Turn right," I said. "Way right."

I felt the airplane bank as she turned. Now I saw luminous threads, one thin strand of fog stretched vertically, another horizontal. We were to the left of where they crossed, approaching center.

"OK. Roll out."

The cross drifted lower, began to focus. "Start down. Left a little. . . ."

Now the picture in my mind was as clear as the needles of an instrument landing approach, and as precise. How real our imagination does seem!

"Down a bit," I said. "We're on glidepath, on centerline. A little more left. We should be about ready to touch; are we?"

"Another few feet," said Leslie.

"OK. Now. Power off," I said.

I heard waves brushing the keel of our flying-boat, opened my eyes to watch the world disappear, wrapped in spray. Then everything turned moving black, dim silver shapes shuddering by in the dark until we stopped.

We stood on a wide field of concrete . . . an air base! Blue taxiway lights at the edges, runways in the distance, jet fighter planes tied down, silver in moonlight.

"Where are we?" Leslie whispered.

The fighters, row after row of them, were North American F-86F Sabrejets. All at once I knew where we were. "Williams Air Force Base, Arizona. Fighter Gunnery School. It's 1957," I murmured. "I used to walk out here at night to be with the airplanes."

"Why are we whispering?" she asked.

That moment, an Air Police jeep turned at the end of a row, patrolling, cruised toward us. It slowed, curved around an airplane parked to our right and stopped.

We couldn't see the AP, but we could hear his voice.

"Excuse me, sir," he said, "would you mind showing me your identification?"

There was a low voice, a few syllables we couldn't catch.

"It's me he's talking to," I told Leslie. "I remember this. . . ."

"Certainly, sir," came the voice. "We're just checking. There's no problem."

A moment later the jeep backed to clear the wing, dropped into low gear, gunned its engine, swung around the airplane. If the driver saw us, he gave no sign. Before we could dodge, the headlights were glaring suns exploding toward us.

"WATCH OUT!" I shouted, too late. Leslie screamed.

The jeep rammed us head-on, ran through us without a second thought and drove off, still accelerating.

"Oh," I said, "I forgot. Sorry."

"It is hard to get used to!" she said breathlessly.

A figure appeared at the wing of the airplane. "Who's there? Are you all right?"

He wore a dark nylon flight suit and jacket, a dim ghost himself in the moonlight. White embroidered pilot's wings on the jacket, yellow second-lieutenant's bars.

"You go," Leslie whispered. "I'll stay here." I nodded, gave her a hug.

"I'm fine," I said, walking around the wing toward him. "Permission to join you?" I smiled at myself, sounding cadet-like after all these years.

"Who is it?"

Why must he ask hard questions? "Sir," I answered, "Second Lieutenant Bach, Richard D., A-O-Three-Zero-Eight-Zero-Seven-Seven-Four, sir!"

"Mize, is that you?" he chuckled. "What are you doing out here clowning around?"

Phil Mizenhalter, I thought. What a friend he was! In ten years he'll be dead, shot down with his F-105 in Viet Nam.

"It's not Mize," I said. "It's Richard Bach, it's you from your future, thirty years from tonight."

He peered through the dark. "You're *who*?"

If we do much more of this, I thought, we'd better get used to that question.

"I'm you, Lieutenant. I'm yourself with a little more experience. I'm the one made all the mistakes that you're going to make, and somehow survived."

He walked closer, inspecting me in the dark, still thinking this was a joke. "I'm going to make mistakes?" he said with a smile. "That's hard to believe."

"Call them unexpected learning experiences."

"I think I can handle 'em," he said.

"You've already made the big one," I pressed on. "You joined the military. Smart thing would be to quit now. Not the smart thing. The wise thing would be to quit."

"Ho!" he said. "I just graduated from flight school! I still can't believe I'm an Air Force pilot and you're telling me quit? That's pretty good. What else do you know?" If he thought I was a game, he was willing to play.

"OK," I said, "in the past I remember, I thought I was using the Air Force to learn how to fly. Fact is, the Air Force was using me, and I didn't know it."

"But I do know it!" he said. "I happen to love my country and if there's fighting to be done to keep it free I want to be there!"

"Remember Lieutenant Wyeth? Tell me about Lieutenant Wyeth."

He looked at me sideways, uneasy.

"The name was Wyatt," he corrected. "Instructor in preflight training. Something happened to him in Korea and he went a little crazy. Stood in front of our class and wrote in big letters on the board: *KILLERS!* Then he turned around, his face like grinning death, and he said, *'That's you!'* His name was Wyatt."

"You know what you're going to learn in your future, Richard?" I said. "You're going to find out that Lieutenant Wyatt was the sanest person you'll ever meet in the Air Force."

He shook his head. "You know," he said, "every once in a while I imagine what it would be like to meet you, to talk to the man I'm going to be in thirty years. You're not like him. Not at all! He's proud of me!"

"I'm proud of you too," I said. "But for different reasons than you think. I'm proud because I know you're doing the best you know how to do. I'm not proud that the best you know is to volunteer to kill people, to strafe and rocket and napalm villages full of terrified women and children."

"Like hell I will!" he said. "I'm going to fly air-to-air day fighter defense!"

I didn't say a word.

"Well, air defense is what I'd like to do. . . ."

Just looked at him, in the dark.

"Hey, I'm serving my country and I'll do whatever. . . ."

"You could serve your country ten thousand other ways," I said. "Come on, why are you here? Are you honest enough with yourself even to know?

He hesitated. "I want to fly."

"You knew how to fly before you joined the Air Force. You could have flown Piper Cubs and Cessnas."

"They're not . . . fast enough."

"Not like the pictures on the recruiting posters, are they? Cessnas aren't like the airplanes in the movies."

"No," he said at last.

"So why are you here?"

"There's something about high-performance. . . ." He checked himself, as honest now as he knew how to be. "There's something about fighter planes. There's a glory there nothing else has."

"Tell me about the glory."

"The glory comes from a . . . a mastery of the thing. Flying this airplane. . . ." He patted the wing of the Sabre lovingly. ". . . well, I'm not plodding around in the mud, I'm not tied to desks or buildings or anything on earth. I can go faster than sound, forty thousand feet up—no other living thing has ever been there, practically. Something in me knows we're not ground-creatures, says *we don't have limits,* and the closest I can come to living what I know is true is flying one of these."

Of course. That's why I had wanted the speed and dazzle and flash. I'd never put it in words, never put it in thoughts. Just felt it.

"I hate it when they hang bombs on airplanes," he said. "But I can't help that. Otherwise there wouldn't be any machines like this."

Without you, I thought, war would die. I swept my hand toward the Sabre. To this day I consider it the loveliest airplane that's ever been built. "Beautiful," I said. "Bait."

"Bait?"

"The fighter planes are bait. You're the fish."

"So what's the hook?"

"The hook is going to kill you when you find out," I said. "The hook is that you, Richard Bach, human being, are personally responsible for every man and woman and child that you will kill with this thing."

"Wait a minute! I'm not responsible, I have nothing to do with decisions like that! I follow orders. . . ."

"Orders are no excuse, the Air Force is no excuse, war is no excuse. Every murder will haunt you till you die, every night you'll wake up screaming, killing every one again, over and over."

He stiffened. "Listen, without the Air Force, if we're attacked . . . I'm here to protect our *freedom*!"

"You said you were here because you want to fly, and for the glory."

"My flying protects my country. . . ."

"That's what the others say, too, word for word. The Russian soldiers, the Chinese soldiers, the Arab soldiers, the fill-in-the-blank soldiers of the fill-in-the-blank nation. They learn In Us We Trust. Defend the Motherland, the Fatherland from Them. But their Them, Richard, is *you*!"

His arrogance suddenly disappeared. "Remember the model airplanes?" he said, almost pleading. "A thousand model airplanes, and a tiny me flew in every one. Remember climbing trees, looking down? I was the bird, waiting to fly. Remember throwing yourself from diving boards, pretending it was flight? Remember the first time up, in Paul Marcus' Globe Swift? I wasn't the same for days. I wasn't the same ever!"

"That's the way it's planned," I said.

"Planned?"

"Soon as you learned to see, pictures. Soon as you learned to listen, stories and songs. Soon as you learned to read, books and signs and posters, flags and movies and statues and tradition, classes in history, pledge allegiance, salute the flag. There is Us and there is Them. Them will hurt us if we're not vigilant, suspicious, angry, armed. Follow orders, do as you're told, defend your country.

"Encourage the boy-children's curiosity in machines that

move: automobiles, ships, airplanes. Now set before them the most excellent of these magical machines in one place: in the military, in the armed forces of every country in the world. Hulk the auto-drivers in million-dollar tanks, launch the sea-lovers to command nuclear cruisers, offer the would-be flyers, offer you, Richard, the fastest airplanes in history, all your very own, and you get to wear this flashy helmet and visor and paint your name on the side of the cockpit!

"They lead you on: *Are you good enough? Are you tough enough?* They praise you: *Elite! Top gun!* They drape you in flags, pin you with wings on your pocket, bars on your shoulders, bright-ribbon medals for doing just as you are told by the ones who pull your strings.

"There are no-truth-in-advertising rules for recruiting posters. The pictures show jets. They don't say 'By the way, if you're not killed flying this airplane, you'll die on the cross of your personal responsibility for the people you kill with it.'

"This is not dumb others, Richard, this is *you*, eating the bait and proud of it. Proud as a grand free marlin in your handsome blue uniform, hooked on this airplane, hauled by the line toward your own death, your own grateful proud honorable patriotic pointless stupid death.

"And the United States won't care, and the Air Force won't care, and the general who gives the orders won't care, either. The only one who is ever going to care that you killed the people you're going to kill is you. You and them and their families. Some glory, Richard. . . ."

I turned and walked away, left him at the wing of the fighter. Are lives so destined by *indoctrination,* I thought, that there is no changing? Would I change, would I listen to me if I were him?

He didn't raise his voice, or call out after me. He spoke as though he hadn't noticed I had left. "What do you mean, I'm responsible?"

What an odd feeling. I was talking with myself, but his mind was no longer mine to change. We can only transform our lives in the split-second eternity that is our now. If we move one moment from that now, it's somebody else's choice.

I strained to catch his voice. "How many people will I kill?"

I walked back to join him. "In 1962, you'll be sent to Europe with the 478th Tactical Fighter Squadron. It will be called the 'Berlin Crisis.' You will memorize routes to one primary and two secondary targets. There's a pretty good chance, five years from now, that you will drop a hydrogen bomb on the city of Kiev."

I watched him. "Mostly the city is known for its publishing and its film industry, but what will matter to you are the railroad yards in the middle of town and the machine-tool factories at the edge."

"How many people . . . ?"

"There will be nine hundred thousand people in Kiev that winter, and if you follow orders, the few thousand that survive your attack will wish they were dead, too."

"Nine hundred thousand people?"

"Tempers short, national pride at stake, safety of the free world," I said, "one ultimatum after another. . . ."

81

"Will I . . . did you drop the bomb?" He was tense as steel, listening to his future.

I opened my mouth to say no, the Soviets backed down, but my mind went silver with rage. Some alternate me from a different-past holocaust grabbed my neck and spoke fury, a razor voice desperate to get through.

"Of course I did! I didn't question, any more than you question! I thought if there's a war, the President's the one with all the facts, he makes the decisions, he's responsible. I never thought till takeoff that the President can't be responsible for dropping the bomb because *the President doesn't know how to fly an airplane!"*

I struggled to gain control, lost.

"The President doesn't know a missile-launch key from a rudder-pedal, the Commander in Chief can't start the engine, he can't taxi to the runway—without me he'd be one harmless fool in Washington and the world would muddle along without his nuclear war. But Richard, that fool had *me!* He didn't know how to kill a million people, *so I did it for him!* The bomb wasn't his weapon, *I* was his weapon! I never put it together then: a handful of us in the world know how, and without us there could be no war! I destroyed Kiev, can you believe this, I incinerated nine hundred thousand people because some crazy . . . *told me to do it!"*

The lieutenant stood mouth open, watching me.

"Did the Air Force teach you ethics?" I hissed. "Ever have a class called *Accountability of Fighter Pilots*? You never had, and you never will! The Air Force says follow orders, do as you're told: your country, right or wrong. It doesn't tell you that what you've got to live with is your *conscience*, right or wrong. You follow your orders to burn Kiev and six hours later a fellow you'd really like, a pilot named Pavel Chernov, follows his orders and cremates Los Angeles. Everybody dies. If you murder yourself when you kill the Russians, *why kill 'em at all?*"

"But I . . . I promised to follow orders!"

At once the madman let go my throat in despair and disappeared. I tried reason once more.

"What will they do to you if you spare a million lives, if you don't follow orders?" I asked. "Call you a non-professional pilot? Court-martial you? Kill you? Would that be worse than what you would have done to the city of Kiev?"

He looked at me for a long moment in silence. "If you could tell me anything," he said finally, "and I'd promise to remember, what would you say? That you're ashamed of me?"

I sighed, suddenly weary. "Oh, kid, it'd be a lot easier on me if you'd just shut your mind and insist you're right, following orders. Why do you have to be such a nice guy?"

"Because I'm you, sir," he said.

I felt a touch on my shoulder, and I looked up to the sheen of golden hair in moonlight.

"Introduce me?" said Leslie. Shadows showed a sorceress in the night.

I straightened at once, catching a glimmer of what she intended.

"Lieutenant Bach," I said, "meet Leslie Parrish. Your soulmate, your wife-to-be, the woman you've been looking for, the one you'll find at the end of many adventures, at the beginning of the best."

"Hello," she said.

"I . . . ah . . . hello," he faltered. "You say . . . my *wife?*"

"That time may come," she said softly.

"Are you sure you mean me?"

"There's a young Leslie this moment," she said, "starting her career, wondering who you are, where you are, when you're going to meet. . . ."

The young man was starstruck at the sight of her. For years he had dreamed her, loved her, knew she waited somewhere in the world for him.

"I can't believe this," he said. "You're from my future?"

"One of your futures," she said.

"But how can we meet, where are you now?"

"We can't meet till you're out of the military. In some futures, we'll never meet at all."

"But if we're soulmates, we have to meet!" he said. "Soulmates are born to spend their lives together!"

She stepped back from him, a small step. "Maybe not."

Never has she looked more lovely than she does tonight, I thought. How much he wants to fly across time to find her!

"I didn't think anything could . . . what power is there that can keep soulmates apart?" he said.

Was it my wife speaking, or an alternate Leslie from her own different time?

"My dearest Richard," she said, "in that future when you bomb Kiev, and your Russian friend, the flier, bombs Los Angeles? The studio at Twentieth Century-Fox, where I'll be working, is less than a mile from ground zero. I'll be dead a second after the first bomb falls."

She turned to me, a flash of terror in her eyes, the purpose of our lives together lost. There are some futures, cried that other self . . . soulmates don't always meet!

I was with her at once, my arm around her, holding her while the terror passed. "We can't change it," I said.

She nodded, anguish gone, knowing before I did. "You're right," she said sadly, and turned her face to the lieutenant. "It's not our choice. It's yours."

The best we could say, we had said. The best we knew, he knew.

Somewhere in our simultaneous future, Leslie did as Pye had said. The moment to leave had come, and closing her eyes, imagining the world of the pattern, she pressed the throttle of the Seabird forward.

The night sky and the fighter planes and the air base shuddered about us, the lieutenant himself saying *wait . . . !*

And gone.

Dear God, I thought. Women and children and men, lovers and bakers, actresses and musicians and comedians and doctors and librarians, the lieutenant would kill them all, no mercy, when some President orders. Puppies and birds and trees and flowers and fountains, books and museums and paintings, he'll burn his own soulmate to death and nothing we can say will stop him. He's *me*, and I can't stop him!

Leslie read my mind, held my hand. "Richard, sweetheart, listen. Maybe we couldn't have stopped him," she said. "But maybe we did."

$\mathcal{L}$eslie held the throttle forward, eased the Seabird into the sky. A hundred feet above the pattern she pulled back to cruise power, trimmed the machine for level.

Though we flew through bright sky above bright water, despair hung dark and heavy in the cockpit, astonishment that intelligent human beings could be drawn into war. It was as if the idea were brand new to us, our grim acceptance of the possibility in our day-to-day lives shattered by a fresh look at the madness of it.

"Pye," I said at last, "of all the places we could land in a pattern that goes to infinity, why did we pick these pasts? Why Leslie at the piano, Richard at his fighter plane?"

"Can you guess?" she asked, glancing the question to both of us.

I scanned the two events. What did they have in common? "They were both young and lost?"

"Perspective?" Leslie suggested. "Both of them had reached the moment when they needed to remember the power of choices. . . ."

Pye nodded. "Twice right."

"And the purpose of this trip," I said, "is to learn perspective?"

"No," she said, "there is no purpose. You fell here by coincidence."

"Oh, Pye!" I said.

"You don't believe in coincidence? Then you must believe that you're responsible, that you navigated to this place."

"Well, I sure wasn't navigating. . . ." I said. The words sank in, and I turned to look at Leslie.

It was a private joke between us that Leslie, who has no sense of direction on the ground, knows her way better than I do once we're in the air.

"I'm the navigator," she said, and smiled.

"She thinks she's kidding," said Pye. "But you couldn't have made it without her, Richard. Do you know that?"

I nodded. "I'm the one fascinated with ESP and out-of-body travel and near-death experiences," I said. "I read the books, study page after page into the night. Leslie hardly ever reads the books, but she reads minds, sees our future. . . ."

"Richard, I do not! I'm a skeptic and you know it! I've always been a skeptic about your other-world. . . ."

"Always?" said Pye.

"Well . . . I've learned that sometimes he's right," said Leslie. "He comes up with some outlandish idea and next week or next year science discovers the same thing. So I've learned to treat these notions of his, no matter how crazy they seem, with a certain amount of respect. And I'd love the strange twists and turns his mind takes even if science never agreed with him, because he has a fascinating point of view. But I've always been the practical one. . . ."

"Always?" I asked.

"Oh . . . that doesn't count," she said, reading my mind. "I was a little girl. And I didn't like that sort of thing so I stopped it!"

"Leslie's saying that she was gifted with intuition so intense that she frightened herself," said Pye, "so she blocked her gift and does her best to keep it blocked. Practical skeptics do not like to frighten themselves with strange powers."

"My own dear navigator," I said. "No wonder! It wasn't you who wanted to go back when Los Angeles disappeared, it was me. It's not me who can push the throttle forward on a seaplane I can't see, it's you!"

"Don't be silly," Leslie protested. "I'd never be flying a seaplane, I'd never be flying at all if it weren't for you! And the trip to Los Angeles was your idea. . . ."

That was true. I was the one who had tempted Leslie from home and flowers with the invitation to Spring Hill. But ideas are life to us — growth and joy, stress and release. From nowhere come tantalizing questions, exciting answers dancing ahead, urging us to puzzle this out, express that somehow, go here, do this, help there. Neither one of us can resist ideas.

All at once I wondered if we could find out why.

"Pye, where do ideas come from?" I asked.

"Left ten degrees," she said.

"Pardon?" I said. "No, *ideas*. They just . . . appear at the strangest times. Why?"

"The answer to any question you can ask is in the pattern," she said. "Make that twenty degrees to the left, now, and land."

I felt the same about our advanced friend as I had once felt about flight instructors — as long as they were with me in the airplane I wasn't afraid to try any stunt they asked.

"OK, wookie?" I asked my wife. "Are you ready for more?"

She nodded, eager for another adventure.

I turned the amphibian as Pye had asked, checked wheels up flaps down, pulled the power back.

"Two degrees right, line up with that bright yellow stripe underwater straight ahead . . . touch the power just a bit," said our guide. "Here! Perfect!"

∞

The place we stopped looked like overtime in hell. Flames roiled and boomed in furnaces, monster kettles of molten stuff strained aloft on traveling cranes, swung ponderous across a cluttered steel plain four acres under roof.

"Oh, dear. . . ." I said.

An electric flatbed the size of a golf-cart rolled to the aisle nearest us and a slender young woman in coveralls and hard-hat stepped off, heading our way. If she called hello, the word was lost in the clank and roar of iron and fire. A cauldron tilted, a tornado-scream of green sparks burst from the ingot-molds behind her, turning her to silhouette as she walked swiftly toward us.

She was a delicate little thing, blonde curls under her hard-hat, intense blue eyes.

"Quite a spot, isn't it?" she said for introduction, shouting over the noise. She spoke as though she were proud of the place. "You probably don't need these," she said, handing us hard-hats, "but if management catches us without 'em. . . ." She grinned and drew her finger wickedly across her throat.

"But we can't touch. . . ." I began.

She shook her head. "It's OK. You can here."

Sure enough, not only could we touch the hard-hats, they fit. She motioned us to follow.

I glanced at Leslie: who is this? She knew my thought, shrugged, shook her head I don't know.

"Say, what's your name?" I called.

The young woman stopped for a second, surprised. "You have so many names for me, all so formal!" She shrugged and smiled. "Call me Tink."

She led us briskly toward a ramp at the near side of the giant place, a tour-guide along the way. "Now, the ore comes down the belts to the sifters outside," she said, "then it's washed on its way to the main hopper. . . ."

Leslie and I looked questions at each other. Were we supposed to know what was going on?

". . . dumped into one of the crucibles—there are twenty-five on this floor—and heated three thousand degrees. Then an overhead picks it up and brings it down here."

"What are you talking about?" I asked.

"If you'll hold your questions till later," she said, "I'll probably answer most of them along the way."

"But we don't. . . ."

She pointed. "On the traveler," she said, "xenon gas is infused through the melt, then the pour is made into these molds, which are coated twenty microns in powdered chondrite." She smiled, held up a hand, anticipating our question. "No, the chondrite's not to trigger the crystal, it makes it easier to get the ingots out of the molds!"

The ingots were not steel but glass of some kind, turning from orange to lucent white as they cooled.

Alongside were teams of industrial robots trimming near-invisible blocks into beams and cubes and rhomboids, the way cutters trim diamonds into angles and facets.

"The blocks are faced and energized here," said Tink as we hurried by, "each one different, of course. . . ."

Our mystery-guide marched us up a curving ramp into an airlock. "And this is the finish floor," she said, prouder than ever. "This is what you've been waiting to see!"

Doors slid open as we approached, closed behind us when we passed.

The din was gone, the place quiet as destiny, as ordered and as clean. There were felt-top workbenches from one towering wall to the next, and on each table rested a shape of polished crystal, more silent art than heavy industry. People worked carefully, wordless at their tables. The clean room at Spaceship Assembly?

We slowed and stopped by a table where a burly young man sat at a swivel chair in front of what appeared to be an ultra-modern turret-lathe, inspecting a crystal block bigger than I was. The mass was so transparent that it was barely visible, a suggestion in space, yet its planes and angles sparkled fascination. Within the crystal we could see an intricate structure of colored light, minilasers embedded, a dainty network of glowing filaments. The man pressed keys at the machine, and subtle shifts happened in the glass.

I touched Leslie, pointed to the block and nodded perplexed, trying to remember. Where had we seen these before?

"He's checking to see that every connection's finished," Tink said, her voice a hushed murmur now. "One loose filament and the whole unit fails."

The man turned at her words, saw us watching. "Hello!" he said, warm as an old friend. "Welcome!"

"Hello," we answered.

"Do we know you?" I said.

He smiled, and I liked him at once. "Know me, yes. Remember me, probably not. Name's Atkin. Once I was your aircraft rigger, once your Zen master. . . . Oh, I don't suppose you remember." He shrugged, not bothered at all.

I stumbled for words. "What . . . what are you doing here?"

"Take a peek." He pointed to a binocular eyepiece mounted near the crystal. Leslie peered in.

"Oh, my!" she said.

"What?"

"It's . . . it's not glass, Richie. It's ideas! It's like a spiderweb, they're all connected!"

"Tell me."

"It's not in words," she said. "You have to put it in words however you can, I guess."

"What words would you use? Try it on me."

"Oh," she said, fascinated, "look at *that*!"

"Speak," I said. "Please."

"OK, I'll try. It's about . . . how hard it is to make the right choices, and how important it is to stick to the best we know . . . and that we really *do* know what the best is!" She apologized to Atkin. "I know I'm not doing it justice. Would you read this silver section to us?"

Atkin smiled again. "You're doing very well," he said, peering into another eyepiece. "It says: *A tiny change today brings us to a dramatically different tomorrow. There are grand rewards for those who pick the high hard roads, but those rewards are hidden by years. Every choice is made in the uncaring blind, no guarantees from the world around us.* And next to that, see? *The only way to avoid all frightening choices is to leave society and become a hermit, and that is a frightening choice.* And that's connected to: *Character comes from following our highest sense of right, from trusting ideals without being sure they'll work. One challenge of our adventure on earth is to rise above dead systems — wars, religions, nations, destructions — to refuse to be a part of them, and express instead the highest selves we know how to be.*"

"Oh, Richie, listen to this," said Leslie, still gazing into the crystal. *"No one can solve problems for someone whose problem is that they don't want problems solved!* Did I get that one right?" she asked Atkin.

"Perfect!" he said.

She looked back to the crystal, pleased to begin to understand. *"No matter how qualified or deserving we are, we will never reach a better life until we can imagine it for ourselves and allow ourselves to have it.* God knows that's true!

"It's what an idea looks like when you close your eyes and think about it!" She smiled admiration at Atkin. "The whole thing is there, all the connections, every answer to every question you can ask about it. You can follow the connections any way you want. It's brilliant!"

"Thank you," said Atkin.

I turned to our guide. "Tink?"

"Yes?"

"Ideas come from a foundry? From a *steel mill*?"

"They can't be air, Richard," she said earnestly, "we can't use cotton-candy! A person trusts her life to what she believes. Her ideas have to support her, they have to take the weight of her own questions and the weight of a hundred or a thousand or ten thousand critics and cynics and destroyers. Her ideas have to stand the stress of every consequence they bring!"

I shook my head at the expanse of the room, the hundred tables. It's true that our best ideas have always come to us complete and finished, but I was not ready to accept that they came from a. . . .

"It's bad enough to fail when we let go of what we believe," said Tink, "but it's worse when the ideas we've been living by turn out to be wrong." She frowned at me, pure and resolute. "Of course ideas come from a foundry! And not steel. Steel would bend."

"This is wonderful!" said Leslie, absorbed in the crystal again, peering like a submarine commander into the eyepiece. "Listen to this: *Commerce is idea and choice expressed. Look about you this moment: everything you see and touch was once invisible idea until someone chose to bring it into being.*

What a thought! *We can't give money to a needy alternate us in other beliefs of space and time, but we can give ideas which they can turn to fortunes if they choose.* Wookie, come see!"

She gave me her place at the eyepiece and turned to Atkin. "I am astounded!" she said. "It's so . . . precise in there, so well thought out!"

"We do our best," he said modestly. "This one is a challenge. It's a core idea — it's called *Choices* — and if a core idea has flaws, you've got to stop everything in your life till you get it sorted out. Our job is not to stop you, it's to help you move along."

His voice faded as I put my eye to the scope, so completely did the designs inside the crystal take my attention.

They were at once eerie and familiar. Eerie that the matrix of lightbeams and iridescent planes changed from color at once into thought. Familiar because I was sure I had seen this before, watched the same view behind closed eyes, struck by meteor ideas.

How we throw nets at ideas, I thought. In every language, from Arabic to Zulu to calligraphy to shorthand to math to music to art to wrought stone, everything from the Unified Field Theory to a curse to a sixpenny nail to an orbiting satellite, anything expressed is a net around some idea.

A violet glow caught my eye. I spoke the idea aloud as best I could. *"Bad things are not the worst things that can happen to us. NOTHING is the worst thing that can happen to us!"* I checked with Atkin. "Am I close?"

"Word for word," he answered.

Back in the crystal, violet melted to indigo, under the lens. *"An easy life doesn't teach us anything. In the end it's the learning that matters: what we've learned and how we've grown."*

"You've got it," said Atkin.

There was an emerald line in one face, arrowing through the sheet of diamond: *"We can have excuses, or we can have health, love, longevity, understanding, adventure, money, happiness. We design our lives through the power of our choices. We feel most helpless when we've made choices by default, when we haven't designed our lives on our own. That's what you told young Leslie!"*

A third level connected the two planes, seemed to reinforce the structure. *"We are each given a block of marble when we begin a lifetime, and the tools to shape it into sculpture."* Floating parallel: *"We can drag it behind us untouched, we can pound it to gravel, we can shape it into glory."* Parallel next: *"Examples from every other life are left for us to see, lifeworks finished and unfinished, guiding and warning."* Cross-connecting last to first: *"Near the end, our sculpture is nearly finished, and we can smooth and polish what we started years before. We can make our greatest progress then, but to do it we must see past the appearances of age."*

I watched, absorbed as a hummingbird deep in flower, lapsed into silence.

We generate our own environment. We get exactly what we deserve. How can we resent the life we've created for ourselves? Who's to blame, who's to credit, but us? Who can change it, any time we wish, but us?

I swiveled the eyepiece, found corollaries layered at every new angle.

Any powerful idea is absolutely fascinating and absolutely useless until we choose to use it.

Of course, I thought. The exciting thing about ideas is putting them to work. The moment we try them on our own, launch them away from shore, they switch from what-if to become daring plunges down white rivers, as dangerous and as exhilarating.

The moment I turned away from the eyepiece the crystal block on the table changed to artful curiosity. I felt its warm potential, but I lost my grasp of what it meant, of the excitement and power waiting to be used. If it were an idea in mind, there could be no shaking it away.

". . . as stars and comets and planets attract dust with gravity," Atkin was saying to Leslie, happy to talk with someone so fascinated with his work, "so are we centers of thought, attracting ideas all sizes and weights, from flashes of intuition to systems so complex they take lifetimes to explore."

He turned to me. "Done?"

I nodded, and without so much as a fare-thee-well he touched a key on his machine and the crystal vanished. He read my face. "Not vanished," he said. "Different dimension."

"As long as you're here," said Tink, "is there anything you'd like to pass along to another aspect of yourselves?"

I blinked. "What do you mean?"

"What have you learned to give a different you to build on? If you wanted to change a life, let someone unwrap a gift of thought from you, what would it be?"

A maxim sprang to mind. *"There's no disaster that can't become a blessing, and no blessing that can't become a disaster."*

Tink glanced at Atkin, smiled at him proudly. "What a dear thought," she said. "Has it worked for you?"

"Has it worked?" I said. "Worn the paint off it, we've used it so much! We don't judge good and bad nearly so fast as we used to. Our disasters have been some of the best things that ever happened to us. And what we swore were blessings have been some of the worst!"

"What's best and worst?" Atkin asked, casually.

"Best makes us long-term happy, worst makes us long-term sorry."

"How long is long-term?"

"Years. A lifetime."

He nodded, said no more.

"Where *do* you get your ideas?" said Tink. She asked with a smile, but behind it I sensed the question was terribly important to her.

"You won't laugh?"

"Unless it's funny."

"The sleep fairy," I said. "We get our ideas when we're sound asleep, or when we're just waking up and can hardly see to write."

"Then there's the shower fairy," said Leslie, "and the walk fairy and the long-drive fairy, the swim fairy and the gardening fairy. The best ideas come at the most unlikely times, when we're soaking wet or covered with mud or we don't even have a note pad, whenever it's hardest for us to write them down. But they matter so much to us, that we manage to hang on to nearly every one. If we ever meet the idea fairy, the little darling, we're going to hug her flat, we love her so."

With that, Tink covered her face with her hands and burst into tears. "Oh, thank you thank you!" she sobbed. "I work so hard to help . . . I love you, too!"

I was stunned. *"You're the idea fairy?"*

She nodded, her face hidden still.

"Tink runs this place," said Atkin quietly, re-setting his machine parameters to zero. "Takes the job very seriously."

The young woman wiped her eyes with her fingertips. "I know you call me those silly names," she said, "but you listen anyway. You wonder why the more ideas you use, the more you get? Because the idea fairy knows that she matters to you! And as she matters to you, so you matter to her. I tell everybody here we've got to give our very best because these ideas aren't just floating around zerospace, they're getting through!" She reached for her handkerchief. "I'm sorry about the tears. I don't know what came over me. Atkin, I want you to forget this. . . ."

He stared at her, unsmiling. "Forget what, Tink?"

She turned to Leslie, rushed to explain. "You've got to know there's not a person on this floor who isn't a thousand times wiser than I am. . . ."

"The word is *charm,*" said Atkin. "We've all been teachers, we like this work and we have moments when we're not too clumsy with it, but none of us is so charming as Tink. Without charm, the best idea in the universe is dead glass, nobody'll touch it. But you get an idea from the sleep fairy, it's so charming you can't resist, and out into life it goes, changing worlds."

Both of these people can see us, I thought, so they must be an alternate us, aspects who chose different paths in the pattern. Still it was incredible. The idea fairy is *us*? Can different levels of ourselves be spending lifetimes making knowledge crystal clear, hoping we'll see it in our world?

At that moment a machine no larger than a sheepdog hummed alongside, rolling on smooth rubber treads, a blank ingot in its arms. Treads squeaking under the weight, it set the crystal carefully on Atkin's table, released it. Then it beeped twice, softly, backed into the aisle and rolled away whence it had come.

"From this place," I said, ". . . all ideas? Inventions? Answers?"

"Not all," said Tink. "Not the answers you put together from your experience. Just the odd ones that startle and surprise, the ones you stumble across when you're not mesmerized by everyday living. All we do is sift infinite possibilities to find the ones you'd love."

"Story ideas, too?" I asked. "Book ideas? Did *Jonathan Seagull* come from here?"

"The seagull story was perfect for you," she frowned, "but you were a beginning writer and you wouldn't listen."

"Tink, I was listening!"

Her eyes flashed. "Don't tell me you were listening! You

wanted to write, but only if you didn't have to say anything too strange. I had to go wild to get your attention!"

"Wild?"

"It took a psychic experience to do it," said the little soul, reliving her frustration, "and I don't like to resort to that. But if I hadn't shouted the title out loud to you, if I hadn't run the story like a movie in front of your nose, poor Jonathan would have been doomed!"

"You didn't shout."

"Well, I felt like it after all I went through to reach you."

So it had been Tink's voice I'd heard! That dark night so long ago, not shouting but calm as could be: *"Jonathan Livingston Seagull."* Almost scared me to death, hearing the name and nobody there to speak it.

"Thanks for believing in me," I said.

"You're welcome," she said, mollified.

She looked up at me solemnly. "Ideas float all around you but so often you won't see! When you seek inspiration, it's ideas you want. When you pray for guidance, it's ideas that show the way. But you have to pay attention! And it's up to you to put ideas to work!"

"Yes, ma'am," I said.

"Jonathan was the last psychic book-idea you ever got from me, I hope you notice!"

"We don't need fireworks anymore," I told her. "We trust you."

Tink flashed a radiant smile.

Atkin chuckled, turned back to his work table. "Cheero, you two," he said. "Till next time."

"Will we see you again?" Leslie, in her mind, was reaching for the seaplane's throttle.

The director of the idea foundry touched the corner of her eye. "Of course. Meantime I'll tape notes on every thought we send. Remember, don't wake up too fast. And take lots of walks and swims and showers!"

We waved goodbye and the room melted, tumbled away in familiar chaos. Next moment, sure enough, we were in the Seabird once more, lifting from the water, Leslie's hand on the power lever. For the first time since we started this strange adventure, we flew away swept with delight instead of sorrow.

"Pye, what a joy!" said Leslie. "Thank you!"

"I'm glad I could make you so happy before I leave."

"You're leaving?" I asked, suddenly alarmed.

"For a while," she said. "You know how to find the aspects you want to meet, the places of learning for you. Leslie knows how to move on when it's time to go, and you'll know too, Richard, when you learn to trust your inner perception. You hardly need a guide."

She smiled the way flight instructors smile to students before solo. "The possibilities are endless. Let yourselves be drawn to what matters most to you, explore together. We'll meet again."

A smile, a blue-laser flash, and Pye was gone.

9

*I*t doesn't seem as friendly without her, does it?" said Leslie, looking down at the pattern. "Does it look darker to you?"

It did. What had been a sparkling sea had turned forbidding beneath us. Even the colors had changed. The soft pastels and silver-golds had given way to crimsons and burgundies, the paths were charcoal.

I shifted uneasily. "I wish there'd been time for more questions before she left."

"What makes her so sure we can do this by ourselves?" asked Leslie.

"If she's an advanced us," I said, "she ought to know."

"Mm."

"Might as well pick a place and see what happens, don't you think?"

She nodded. "I want to do what Pye said, choose something important, find what matters most." She closed her eyes, concentrating.

Minutes later she opened them. "Nothing! I'm not drawn to anything, isn't that strange? Let me fly and you try it."

At once I felt stiff and tense. It's not fear, I thought, it's caution, simple tension in a twentieth-century human.

I took a deep breath, closed my eyes, relaxed for a moment, then turned desperate to get down. "Power off! Now! Land!"

We stopped in moonlight a few yards from a crude many-angled tent. Its roof was sewn leather, pitch poured along the seams, the walls heavy earth-color cloth turned flickering cherry in the light of sentry torches. From the desert around us came the glimmer of a hundred campfires in the sand, drunken voices rough and loud, the stamp and whicker of horses.

At the entrance to the tent stood two guards we would have taken for centurions were they not so ragged. Scarred, battered, short men in ill-fitting bronze-fastened tunics and helmets, iron-leather boots to keep them from the cold, shortswords and daggers at their sides.

Fire and dark, I shivered. What have I gotten us into?

Watching the guards, I turned my head to Leslie, took her hand. They didn't see us, but what a morsel she'd make if they did!

"Do you have any idea what we're doing here?" I whispered.

"No, sweetie," she whispered back, "it was your landing."

Nearby a fight broke out, men brawling, grappling with each other. No one noticed us.

"I suppose the one we need to see is in the tent," I said.

She glanced at it apprehensively. "If it's an alternate you, there's nothing to worry about, is there?"

"Maybe we don't need to meet this one. I think there's been a mistake. Let's go."

"Richie, maybe this is what's important, what matters most. There must be a reason we're here, something we should learn. Aren't you curious to know what it is?"

"No," I said. I was as curious about the person in the tent as I would be to meet the spider in a hundred-foot web. "I have bad feelings about this."

She hesitated a moment, looked around, troubled. "You're right. One quick peek and we'll go. I just want to see who. . . ."

Before I could stop her, she slipped through the wall of the tent. A second later, I heard her scream.

I raced to follow, saw a beast-figure reaching for her neck, a knife gleaming in its hand.

"NO!"

I leaped forward at the same moment Leslie's attacker fell through her, surprised, his knife clattering softly on the carpet.

The man was low and square and very fast. He caught his weapon before it stopped rolling, vaulted back to his feet, hurled himself at me without a sound. I stepped aside as best I could, but he caught the movement and hit me squarely in the stomach.

I stood there while he passed through my body, a rock through flame, crashed into a tentpost. The post cracked, the ceiling sagged above us.

Knife lost in the crash, the man whirled, shook his head, drew a second dagger from his boot and launched himself in a leaping tackle. He flew through me shoulder-high, landed on a sharp-cornered wooden footstool, demolished a candle-stand.

In a moment he was on his feet again, eyes slits of rage, arms curved toward us like a wrestler's, dagger still in hand. He crept forward, peering, inspecting me. He stood no taller than Leslie's shoulder, but those eyes meant murder.

Suddenly he turned, reached to the collar of Leslie's blouse and ripped downward, a lightning move, looked dumbly at his empty hand.

"Stop!" I shouted.

He whipped around, slashed his knife through my head.

"NO MORE VIOLENCE!"

He stopped, glaring at me. What was frightening about the eyes was not their cruelty but their intelligence. When this man destroyed, it was no accident.

"Can you talk?" I asked, though I didn't expect he'd know English. *"Who are you?"*

He scowled, breathing hard. Then, to my amazement, he answered. Whatever his language, we understood.

He touched his chest. "At-Elah," he said, proudly. "At-Elah, the Scourge of God!"

"At-Elah?" said Leslie. "Attila?"

"Attila the Hun?"

The warrior grinned fiercely at my shock. Then his eyes narrowed again.

"Guard!" he barked.

One of the ruffos from out front was inside at once, fist thumped on chest in salute.

Attila gestured toward us. "You did not tell me I had guests," he said mildly.

The soldier looked terrified, swept his eyes around the room. "But you have no guests, Great One!"

"There is no man in this room? There is no woman?"

"There is no one!"

"That's all. Leave me."

The guard saluted, turned, strode quickly toward the tent flap.

Attila was faster. His hand blurred like a cobra striking, buried the dagger with a pounding thud in the guard's back.

The effect was astonishing, as though the blow had not killed the guard as much as split him in two. The body fell with scarcely a sound in the entryway, while the ghost of the man marched back to his post, unaware that he had died.

Leslie looked at me horrified.

The murderer pulled his dagger from the body.

"Guard!" he called. The other battered tough appeared. "Take this out of here."

We heard the salute, the body dragged away.

Attila walked back to us, slipping the wet knife into the scabbard on his boot.

"Why?" I said.

He shrugged, lifted his head in disdain. "If my guard cannot see what I see in my own tent. . . ."

"No," I said. "Why are you so *vicious?* Why so much murder, so much destruction? Not just this man, but whole cities, whole peoples you destroy, for no reason!"

He was filled with contempt. "Coward! Would you have me ignore the aggressions of an evil empire? Roman imperialists and their lackey puppets? Infidels! God tells me sweep the land of infidels, and I obey God's word!" The eyes glittered. "*'Woe unto you, lands of the West, for I shall set my scourge upon you, yea, the scourge of God shall slay your men; under the wheel of my chariot shall fall your women, and your children under my horse's hoof!'*"

"God's word," I said. "Empty syllables, more powerful than arrows, for no one dares stand against them. How simply the quick grasp power from fools!"

He looked wide-eyed at me. "You speak *my* words!"

"First turn merciless," I went on, shocked at what I was saying, "then claim you're the Scourge of God and your armies swell with those too dim to imagine a loving God, too frightened to challenge an evil one. Shout that God promises women, oranges, wine, all the gold of Persia when they die with the blood of infidels on their swords, and you have a force that turns cities to rubble. To seize power, call up God's word, for that word best shifts fear to rage at any enemy you choose!"

We stared at each other, Attila and I. They *were* his words. They had also been mine. He knew it, and so did I.

How easy it had been to see myself in Tink and Atkin and their world of gentle creativity, how hard it was now to see me in this churn of hatred. So long had I carried the ancient fighter caged within, chained in his portable dungeon, that I refused to know him when I met him face to face.

He turned his back to me, walked a few steps away, stopped. He could not kill us, he could not make us leave. His only alternative was to prevail in mind. He whirled back, scowling.

"I am feared as God is feared!" he warned.

What happens to intelligence when it believes the lies it invents for others? Does it go to mad whirlpools, down midnight drains?

111

Leslie spoke at last, sadness in her voice. "If you believe that power comes from fear," she said, "you lock yourself in with those who deal in fear. It's not a very bright crowd, and what a foolish choice for a man with your mind! If only you'd use that mind for. . . ."

"WOMAN!" he roared. "Be *silent!*"

"You are feared by those who honor fear," she said softly. "You could be loved by those who honor love."

He righted his chair, sat facing me, his back to Leslie, bitter anger in every line of his face as he quoted his scripture. "God says, *'I shall bring low your high towers and your walls to ruin, and no stone of your city shall stand upon another!'* Those are God's orders. I have no orders to love."

If rage could boil, this man was its cauldron. "I hate God," he said, "I hate what He commands. But no other God will speak!"

We didn't answer.

"Your God of love, never does He raise His sword against me, never does He show His face!" He sprang to his feet, lifted the massive chair in one hand and hurled it down, the wood dissolving in splinters. "If He is so mighty, *why does He not stand in my way?*"

Anger is fear, I knew. Every angry person is a frightened one, dreading some loss. And never had I seen a person so angry as this mirror of my own savage fighter, my locked-and-barred inner self.

"Why are you so frightened?" I asked.

He stalked me, fire in his eyes. "You DARE!" he said. "You DARE! to call At-Elah *frightened!* I shall have you cut in pieces and fed to the jackals!"

I clenched my fists in despair. "But you can't touch me, At-Elah! You can't hurt me, and I can't hurt you—I am your own spirit come two thousand years from your future!"

"You cannot hurt me?" he said.

"No!"

"You would if you could!"

"No."

He thought about that for a moment. "Why not? I am Death, the Scourge of God!"

"Please," I said, "no more lies! *Why are you so frightened?*"

Had the chair not been in pieces, he would have smashed it again. *"Because I am alone in an insane world!"* he bellowed. "God is *wicked,* God is *cruel!* And I must be cruelest of all to be king. God commands: kill or die!"

Then all at once he sighed heavily, his fury passed. "I'm alone with monsters," he said, so softly we could barely hear. "Nothing makes sense. . . ."

"It's too sad," said Leslie, anguish on her face. "No more." She turned and walked through the wall of the tent.

I stayed a moment, watching him. This was one of the most savage men in history, I thought. He'd have killed us if he could. Why was I sorry for him?

I followed Leslie, found her standing in the desert some distance from the ghost of the guard who'd been murdered. She was unseeing in anguish, he a mass of concern, watching his body loaded on a cart, puzzling out what had happened.

"You can see me, can't you?" he called to her. "I'm not dead, am I, because I'm . . . here! Are you come to take me to paradise? Are you my woman?"

She didn't answer.

"Ready to go?" I asked her.

He whirled at my voice. "NO! Don't take me!"

"Leslie, push the throttle," I said.

"You do it this time," she answered in a weary voice. "I can't think."

"I'm not too good at this, you know."

She seemed not to hear me and stood unmoving, staring across the desert.

I have to try, I thought. I relaxed as best I could in that place, imagined the Seabird around us, reached for the throttle.

Nothing.

Growly, I thought, *GO!*

"Woman," yelled the spirit-Hun, "come here!"

My wife didn't move. After a moment, he clanked toward us, suddenly resolute. Mortals can't touch us, I thought, but can ghosts of barbarian guards?

I moved to stand between him and Leslie. "I can't get us out of here," I said to her, desperate. "You have to do it!"

The guard lunged.

How swiftly we revert when we're threatened! The ancient Attila-mind took over, the wicked skills of the man in the tent were mine. Never defend; when attacked, attack!

I launched myself split-second toward the warrior's face, dropped last instant to smash him below his knees. He was solid, all right, and so was I.

Below the knees is not fair, I thought.

Hell with fair, said that primitive mind.

The man tumbled over me, struggled to his feet a second before I struck him hard as I could, in the back of the neck, from behind.

Gentlemen don't strike from behind.

Kill! the inner brute cheered.

I meant to use my hand like an axe below his chin when the world vaporized around me, reformed into the thundering cockpit of our seaplane on takeoff. Light! Clean sky swept that dark scene gone.

"Richard, stop!" Leslie screamed.

I caught my hand midair before it knocked the altimeter senseless, turned to her, my eyes like a pit-bull's yet. "Are you all right?"

She nodded, shaken, kept her hand on the throttle, eased the Seabird upward. "I didn't know he could touch us."

"He was a ghost and so were we," I said. "That must be the difference."

I slumped exhausted, disbelieving. Attila had turned every one of his choices to hatred and destruction for the sake of a wicked god that didn't exist. *Why?*

We flew in silence for a while, my wheels spinning down from overdrive. Twice now, as modern lieutenant and ancient general, I'd seen myself as a destroyer and I didn't know why. Are the veterans of even a peacetime military haunted by what might have been, by what they could have done?

"Me? *Attila the Hun?*" I said. "And yet, compared with the pilot who incinerated Kiev, Attila was a pussycat!"

Leslie thought for a long moment. "What does it all mean? We know that events are simultaneous, but does *consciousness* evolve? Once in this lifetime you let the government train you to be a killer. Now that would be impossible. You've changed, you've evolved!"

She took my hand. "Maybe Attila's part of me, too, part of everyone who ever held a murderous thought. Maybe that's why we forget other lifetimes when we're born, to get a fresh start, to concentrate on doing a better job this time."

Better job of what, I nearly said, heard *expressing love* before the question made it into words. "You're right."

It felt as if the seaplane were stained, smeared from our last landing. Clean water sparkled below.

"Mind if I splash down for a minute, wash Growly off?"

She looked questions at me.

"Symbolic, I guess."

She kissed my cheek, knowing my thoughts. "Till you find out how to live for somebody else, why don't you be answerable for Richard Bach's life and let Attila be answerable for his?"

We touched the waves at half-power, slowed but didn't stop, the spray fifty miles per hour, fountains of deep-powder snow blasting high-pressure roostertails as I ruddered left and right, driving out the memory of that wicked lifetime.

I eased the throttle back an inch, meaning to let the spray move forward as we slowed. It did, but of course it dropped us into a different world.

10

Where we stopped, grass spread around us like an emerald pond cupped in mountains. Sunset flamed from crimson clouds.

Switzerland, I thought at once, we've landed on a Swiss postcard. Away down in the valley was a sweep of trees, sudden houses, high peaked roofs, a church steeple. There was a cart on the village road, pulled not by tractor or horse but by some kind of cow.

I saw no one nearby, not a path, not a goat-trail. Just this lake of grass, sprinkled with wildflowers, half-circled by snowcapped rocky steeps.

"Now why do you suppose. . . ." I said. "Where are we?"

"France," said Leslie. She said it without thinking, and before I could ask her how she knew, she caught her breath. "Look."

She pointed to a cleft in the rock, where an old man in a coarse brown robe knelt on the ground near a small campfire. He was welding; brilliant yellow-white flickered and danced on the rocks behind him.

"What's a welder doing up here?" I asked.

She watched him for a moment. "He's not welding," she said, as though she were remembering the scene instead of observing it. "He's praying."

She set off toward him and I followed, deciding to stay quiet. As I had seen myself in Attila, was my wife seeing herself in this hermit?

Closer and we saw sure enough, that was no welding torch. No sound, no smoke, it was a flaring sun-color pillar pulsing above the ground less than a yard from the elder.

". . . and to the world shall you give, as you have received," came a gentle voice from the light. "Give to all who yearn to know the truth from whence we come, the reason for our being, and the course that lies ahead on the way to our forever home."

We stopped a few yards behind him, transfixed by the sight. I had seen that brilliance once before in my life, years ago, had been stunned by one accidental glimpse of what to this day I still call *Love*. The light we saw this moment was the same, so radiant it rendered the world a footnote, a dim asterisk.

Then, next instant, the light was gone. Beneath the place where it had been lay a sheaf of golden paper, a scripture in grand calligraphy.

The man knelt silent, eyes closed, unaware of our presence.

Leslie walked forward, reached for the glowing manuscript, picked it up. In this mystical place, her hand did not pass through the parchment.

Expecting runes or hieroglyphics, we found words in English. Of course, I thought. The old man would read them as French, a Persian as Farsi. So it must be with revelation — it's not the language that matters, but the communication of ideas.

You are creatures of light, we read. *From light have you come, to light shall you go, and surrounding you through every step is the light of your infinite being.*

She turned a page.

By your choice dwell you now in the world which you have created. What you hold in your heart shall be true, and what most you admire, that shall you become.

Fear not, nor be dismayed at the appearance that is darkness, at the disguise that is evil, at the empty cloak that is death, for you have picked these for your challenges. They are the stones on which you choose to whet the keen edge of your spirit. Know that ever about you stands the reality of love, and each moment you have the power to transform your world by what you have learned.

The pages went on, hundreds of them. We leafed through, struck in awe.

You are life, inventing form. No more can you die on sword or years than you can die on doorways through which you walk, one room into another. Every room gives its word for you to speak, every passage its song for you to sing.

Leslie looked at me, her eyes luminous. If this writing could touch us so, I thought, we from the twentieth century, what effect would it have on people from the whatever-this-was . . . the twelfth!

We turned back to the manuscript. No words of ritual, no directions for worship, no calling down fire and destruction on enemies, no disasters for unbelievers, no cruel Attila-gods. It didn't mention temples or priests or rabbis or congregations or choirs or costumes or holy days. It was scripture written for the loving inner being, and for that being only.

Turn these ideas loose in this century, I thought, a key to recognize our power over belief, unleash the power of love, and terror will vanish. With this, the world can sidestep the Dark Ages!

The old man opened his eyes, saw us at last, and stood as unafraid as if he'd read the scripture through. He glanced at me, looked a long moment at Leslie.

"I am Jean-Paul Le Clerc," he said. "And you are angels."

Before we recovered from our puzzlement the man laughed, joyfully. "Did you notice," he said, "the Light?"

"Inspiration!" said my wife, handing him the golden pages.

"Inspiration, indeed." He bowed as though he remembered her, and she, at least, were an angel. "These words are key to the truth for any who will read, they are life to those who will listen. When I was a child, the Light promised that the pages would come to my hand on the night you should appear. Now that I am old, you have come, and they."

"They will change the world," I said.

He looked at me strangely. "No."

"But they were given to you. . . ."

". . . in test," he said.

"Test?"

"I have traveled far," he said, "I have studied scriptures of a hundred faiths, from Cathay to the Norselands." His eyes twinkled. "And in spite of my study, I have learned. Every grand religion begins in light. Yet only hearts hold light. Pages cannot."

"But you have in your hands. . . ." I said. "You must read it. It's beautiful!"

"I have paper in my hands," said the elder. "Give these words to the world, and they will be loved and understood by those who already know their truth. But before we give them we must name them. And that will be their death."

"To name a beautiful thing is to kill it?"

He looked at me surprised. "To name a thing is harmless. To name these ideas is to create a religion."

"Why?"

He smiled, handing me the manuscript. "I give these pages to you . . . ?"

"Richard," I told him.

"I give these pages directly from the Light of Love to you, Richard. Do you want to give them in turn to the world, to people yearning to know what they say, to ones who have not been privileged to stand at this place in the moment the gift was given? Or do you want to keep this writing for yourself alone?"

"I want to give them, of course!"

"And what will you call your gift?"

What is he getting at, I wondered. "Does it matter?"

"If you do not name it, others will. They will call it *The Book of Richard.*"

"I see. All right. I'll call it anything . . . the pages."

"And will you safeguard *The Pages*? Or will you allow others to edit them, to change what they don't understand, to strike out what they please, whatever is not to their liking?

"No! No changes. They were delivered from the light! No changes!"

"Are you sure? Not a line here and there, for good reason? 'Most people won't understand?' 'This might offend?' 'The message isn't clear?'"

"No changes!"

He raised his eyebrows, questioning. "Who are you to insist?"

"I was here when they were given," I said. "I saw them appear, myself!"

"So," he said, "you have become the Keeper of the Pages?"

"Doesn't have to be me. It can be anyone, as long as they promise no changes."

"But someone is Keeper of the Pages?"

"Someone. I suppose."

"And here begins the Pageite priesthood. Those who give their lives to protect an order of thinking become the priests of that order. Yet any new order, any new way, is change. And change is the end of the world as it is."

"These pages are no threat," I said. "They're love and freedom!"

"And love and freedom are the end of fear and slavery."

"Of course!" I said, vexed. What was he getting at? Why was Leslie standing silent? Didn't she agree that this was. . . .

"Those who profit from fear and slavery," said Le Clerc, "will they be happy with the message of the Pages?"

"Probably not, but we can't let this . . . light . . . be lost!"

"Will you promise to protect the light?" he said.

"Of course!"

"The other Pageites, your friends, they'll protect it too?"

"Yes."

"And if the profiteers in fear and slavery convince the king of this land that you are dangerous, if they march on your house, if they come with swords, how are you going to protect the Pages?"

"I'll take them away! I'll escape!"

"And when you're followed, and caught, and cornered?"

"If I have to fight, I'll fight," I said. "There are principles more important than life. Some ideas are worth dying for."

The old man sighed. "And so began the Pageite Wars," he said. "Armor and swords and shields and banners, horses and fire and blood in the streets. They will not be small wars. Thousands of true believers will join you, tens of thousands, swift and strong and smart. But the principles of the Pages challenge the rulers of every nation that keeps its power through fear and darkness. Tens of thousands will ride against you."

At last it began to dawn, what Le Clerc was trying to tell me.

"To be known," he went on, "to be distinguished from others, you will need a symbol. What symbol will you choose? What sign will you strike upon your banners?"

My heart sank under the weight of his words, but I struggled on.

"The symbol of light," I said. "The sign of the flame."

"And so shall it be," he said, reading history unwritten, "that the Sign of the Flame shall meet the Sign of the Cross on the battlefields of France, and the Flame shall prevail, a glorious victory, and the first cities of the Cross shall be leveled by your pure fire. But the Cross shall join with the Crescent, and together their armies shall swarm in from the south and the east and down from the north, a hundred thousand armed men to your eighty thousand."

Oh, stop, I wanted to say. I know what comes next.

"And for every soldier of the Cross and warrior of the Crescent whom you kill protecting your gift, a hundred will hate your name. Their fathers and mothers, their wives and daughters and sons and friends will hate the Pageites and the cursed Pages for the murder of their loved ones, and every Pageite will despise every Christian and cursed Cross and every Moslem and cursed Crescent for the murder of their own."

"No!" I cried. Every word he said was true.

"And during the Wars, altars will spring up, cathedrals and spires will rise to enshrine the Pages. Those reaching for growth and understanding will find themselves burdened instead with new superstitions and new limits: bells and symbols, rules and chants, ceremonies and prayers and vestments, incense and offerings of gold. The heart of Pageism will turn from love to gold. Gold to build greater temples, gold to buy swords to convert the non-believers and save their souls.

"And when you die, First Keeper of the Pages, gold to build images of you. There will be towering statues, grand frescoes, paintings to commit this scene to immortal art. See, woven in this tapestry: here the Light, there the Pages, there the vault of the sky opened to Paradise. Here kneels Richard the Great in gleaming armor; here the lovely Angel of Wisdom, the Hallowed Pages in her hand; here old Le Clerc at his humble campfire in the mountains, witness to the vision."

No! I thought. Impossible!

But it wasn't impossible, it was inevitable.

"Give these pages to the world, and there shall be another mighty religion, another priesthood, another Us and another Them, one set against the other. In a hundred years, a million will have died for the words we hold in our hands; in a thousand years, tens of millions. All for this paper."

There was no trace of bitterness in his voice, nor did it grow cynical or weary. Jean-Paul Le Clerc was filled with a lifetime's learning, calm acceptance of what he had found.

Leslie shivered.

"Do you want my jacket?" I said.

"No thank you, wookie," she said. "It's not the cold."

"Not the cold," said Le Clerc. He stooped and picked a brand from his fire, raised it to touch the golden pages. "This will warm you."

"No!" I jerked the sheaf away. "Burn the truth?"

"The truth doesn't burn. The truth waits for anyone who wishes to find it," he said. "Only these pages will burn. It is your choice. Would you like Pageism to become the next religion in this world?" He smiled. "You will be saints of the church. . . ."

I looked to Leslie, saw the horror in her eyes that I felt in my own.

She took the brand from him, touched it to the corners of the parchment. The blaze grew to a wide sun-white blossom under our fingers, and in a moment we let the bright shards fall to the ground. They burned a moment longer and went dark.

The old man sighed his relief. "What a blessed evening!" he said. "How rarely are we given the chance to save the world from a new religion!"

Then he faced my wife, smiling hopefully. "We did save it?"

She smiled back at him. "We did. There is not a word in our history, Jean-Paul Le Clerc, of the Pageites or their wars."

They looked a tender goodbye to each other, skeptic to loving skeptic. Then with a small bow to both of us, the old man turned and walked up the mountain into the dark.

The fiery pages still burned in my mind, inspiration turned to ash.

"But the ones who need what those pages had to say," I said to Leslie. "How can they . . . how can we learn what was written there?"

"He's right," she said, looking after the man until she could see him no more, "whoever wants truth and light can find it for themselves."

"I'm not sure. Sometimes we need a teacher."

She turned to me. "Try this," she said. "Pretend that you honestly truly deeply want to know who you are, where you came from and why you're here. Pretend you're willing never to rest till you know."

I nodded and imagined myself non-stop determined resolute, eager to learn, combing libraries for books and back-issues, haunting lectures and seminars, keeping diaries of my hopes and speculation, writing intuitions, meditating on mountaintops, following leads from dreams and coincidence, asking strangers—all the steps we take when learning matters more than anything. "OK."

"Now," she said, "can you imagine yourself *not finding out?*"

Whuf, I thought. How this woman can make me see!

I bowed in answer. "My Lady Le Clerc, Princess of Knowing."

She curtsied slowly in the dark. "My Lord Richard, Prince of the Flame."

Close and silent in the clear mountain air, I took her in my arms, the stars no longer above but around us. We were one with the stars, one with Le Clerc, with the pages and their love, one with Pye and Tink and Atkin and Attila, one with everything that is, that ever was or will be. One.

ile after mile passed under us as we flew in quiet joy. If only the chance wasn't one in trillions, I thought. If only everyone could fly to this place just once each lifetime!

A luminous coral glow appeared underwater, a magnet to us both, and Leslie banked the Seabird around it.

"It's glorious," she said. "Shall we land?"

"I think so. What does your intuition say? What are we trying to find?"

"What matters most."

I nodded.

∞

We stopped in what I would have sworn was Red Square after dark. Cobblestones beneath us, great floodlit walls towering to our right, gilded onion domes against winter night sky. No question, we were dab in the middle of Moscow without visa or guide.

"Oh, my," I said.

The evening crowd bustled past us in greatcoats and furs, frowning against snowflakes.

"Can you tell where we are from the people?" Leslie asked. "Pretend they're New Yorkers in fuzzy hats, can you tell?"

The place wasn't narrow enough for New York, it lacked the nightstreet fear. Aside from the city, though, when I reached for the difference between these people and Americans, it was hard to tell.

"It's not the hats," I said. "They seem Russian like the-day-after-Thursday seems Friday."

"Could they be Americans?" she asked. "If this were Minneapolis and we saw these people, would we say, *Russians!*" She paused. "Do *I* look Russian?"

I squinted at her, tilted my head. In this Soviet crowd, blue eyes, high cheekbones, golden hair.... "You Russians are some beautiful women!"

"*Spasibo,*" she said demurely.

Suddenly a couple in the crowd stopped, arm in arm, not

twenty feet away, staring at us as though we were tentacled Martians from a black-saucer sky.

The other pedestrians shot them glances for stopping short, swirled around them. The couple paid no attention, their eyes glued to us while their fellow citizens walked heedless through us as though we were invisible holograms projected in the path.

"Hello!" said Leslie, with a little wave.

Nothing. They stared as if they did not understand. Had our strange ability to know any language failed us in the Soviet Union?

"Hello," I tried. "How are you? Are you looking for us?"

The woman was first to recover. Dark hair cascading from under her fur hat, eyes curious, inspecting us. "Are we?" she asked with a bewildered smile. "Then we wish you good evening!"

She moved nearer, bringing the man closer to us than he might have preferred.

"You are Americans," he said.

I hadn't known I was holding my breath till I started to breathe again.

"How can you tell?" I said. "We were just this moment talking about that!"

"You look like Americans."

"What is it about us? Is there something New World about our eyes?"

"Your shoes. We tell Americans by their shoes."

Leslie laughed. "Then how can you tell Italians?"

He hesitated, smiled the smallest of smiles. "You can't tell Italians," he said. "They already know everything. . . ."

We all laughed. How strange, I thought, less than a minute after our meeting, the four of us acting as though we might be friends.

We told them who we were and what had happened, but I guessed it was our queer state of unreality that convinced them we were real. Yet Tatiana and Ivan Kirilov were as fascinated with us for being American as for being their alternate selves.

"Come, please," said Tatiana, "to our home! Is not so far. . . ."

I had always felt that we had chosen Soviets for adversaries because they are so like us, marvelously civilized barbarians. Yet their apartment was not barbaric, it was as warm and bright as we would have made it ourselves.

"Come in," said Tatiana, leading us to the living room. "Please, be comfortable."

A calico kitten drowsed on the sofa. "Hallo, Petrouchka," she said. "Were you good girl today?" She sat next to the cat, moved it to her lap, stroked it gently. Petrouchka blinked at her, curled into a ball, fell back to sleep.

Large windows faced east, waiting for morning sun. Lining the walls opposite were oversize bookshelves, records and tapes of the same music we listen to at home: Bartok, Prokofiev, Bach; Nick Jameson's *A Crowd of One*, Tina Turner's *Private Dancer*. Many books, three shelves on consciousness and dying and extrasensory perception. Of those, I suspected Tatiana hadn't read a one. Missing were the personal computers. How could they live without computers?

Ivan, we learned, had been an aeronautical engineer, a member of the Party, and he'd risen quite some way in the Ministry of Aviation.

"Relative wind doesn't care if we fly Soviet wing or United States wing," he said. "Exceed critical angle of attack and we stall, don't we?"

"Not American wings," I told him straightfaced. "American wings never stall."

"Oh, those," he said, nodding. "Yes, we tried your non-stalling wings. But we never found a way to board passengers into airplane that couldn't land! We had to catch American wings with nets, send them back to Seattle. . . ."

Our wives weren't listening. "Last twenty years I went crazy!" said Tatiana. "Government didn't want anything to work too well. If it's less efficient, they think it makes more work to keep everyone busy. *I* say, it's too much *bureaucracy*! We don't have to live with this mess. Especially in film bureau, our job is communicating! Well, they laugh and say Tatiana, you stay calm. But now comes perestroika, comes glasnost, and things move!"

"Now you don't have to stay calm?" asked her husband.

"Vanya," she said, "now I can do my best, I can *simplify*. I am very calm!"

"We wish we could simplify our government," said Leslie.

"Your government is starting to look like ours, which is great," I said, "but ours is starting to look like yours, which is terrible!"

"Better we look like each other than smash each other," said Ivan. "But have you seen newspapers? We cannot believe your President has spoken these words!"

"About the Evil Empire?" said Leslie. "That President did turn a little dramatic in his speeches. . . ."

"No," said Tatiana. "Calling us names was silly, but that was long ago. Now today, read!" She found the paper, scanned for the quote. "Here." She read to us. "*'The temporary stain of radiation on foreign soil is better than the permanent stain of Communism on the minds of American children,'* said the capitalist leader. *'I am proud of the courage of my fellow citizens, and grateful for their prayers, and I pledge, under God and according to His will, to lead freedom to its final victory!'*"

My blood ran cold. When the God of hatred appears, look out!

"Oh, come on," said Leslie. "Temporary radiation? Freedom's final victory? What is he talking about?"

"He says he has great public support," said Ivan. "Do people of America want to destroy people of Soviet Union?"

"Of course not," I said. "That's the way Presidents talk. They always say they have the full support of the people, and unless there's a mob screaming and throwing rocks at the White House on the evening news, they hope we'll believe it."

"Our little world was growing up," said Tatiana. "Lately we come to think we spend too much defending ourselves from Americans, but now . . . to us these words are insane! Instead of too much for defense maybe we spend not enough. How do we get off this terrible . . . this treadmill never stops! We all run and run, who knows when is enough?"

"What if you inherited a house you'd never seen before," I said. "And one day you go to visit your house and find the windows are all filled with. . . ."

"Guns!" said Ivan, astonished. How could an American know the same metaphor a Russian had invented for himself? "Machine guns and cannons and missiles, pointing across field toward another house not so far away. And that house has windows all filled just the same, with cannons pointing back! These houses have enough guns to kill each other a hundred times! What would we do if we inherited such a house?"

He gestured palm up for me to take the story if I could.

"Live with guns and call it peace?" I said. "Buy more guns because the man in the other house buys more guns? Paint's falling off our walls, the roof's leaking, but our guns are oiled and aimed!"

"Is the neighbor more likely to shoot if we take the guns out of our windows," said Leslie, "or if we put more in?"

"If we took a *few* guns from our window," Tatiana replied, "so we can kill him only ninety times, will that make him shoot because he is stronger than we are? I don't think so. So, I remove one old, small—gun."

"Unilaterally, Tatiana?" I said. "No treaty? No years of negotiations? You're going to *disarm unilaterally* while he has all these cannons and rockets pointed at your bedroom?"

She tossed her head in defiance. "Unilaterally!"

"Do that," her husband nodded agreement, "then ask the man to tea. And you serve him a little pastry and you mention to him, 'Listen, I just inherited this house from uncle, as you inherited yours. Maybe they didn't like each other, but I have no quarrel with you. Does your roof leak like mine does?'"

He folded his hands in front of him. "What does the man do? Does he eat our pastry, then go home and shoot us?" He turned and smiled at me. "Americans are crazy, Richard. Are you that crazy? After eating our pastry, *you will go home and shoot us?"*

"Americans are not crazy," I said, "we are crafty."

He looked at me sideways.

"You're convinced that America is spending billions on missiles and high-tech guidance systems? Not so. We are *saving* billions. *How,* you ask?" I looked him in the eye, not a smile.

"How?" he asked.

"Ivan, our missiles have no guidance systems! We don't even put engines in them. Only warheads. The rest is cardboard and paint. Long before Chernobyl, we were smart enough to know: *it doesn't matter where the warheads go off!"*

He looked at me, solemn as a judge. *"It doesn't matter?"*

I shook my head. "We crafty Americans realized two facts.

First, we knew that wherever we put a missile silo we weren't building a launch site, we were building an *impact* site! As soon as we turn the first shovel of dirt for the place, we know you have it targeted for five hundred megatons. Second, Chernobyl was a little tiny nuclear accident on the other side of the world, not one hundredth of one warhead, but six days later we were dumping milk in Wisconsin, straining out your gamma rays!"

The Russian arched a heavy eyebrow. "So you realized. . . ."

I nodded. "With ten million megatons to explode against each other, who cares where they go off? Everybody dies! Why spend billions for rockets and computers? First Soviet missile launched against us, we'll fix you . . . we'll blow up New York and Texas and Florida, and you're doomed! Meanwhile, you go broke building missiles." I looked at him, sly as a coyote. "Where do you think we got the money to build Disneyland?"

Tatiana watched me open-mouthed.

"Top secret," I told her. "My old Air Force pals are generals now, Strategic Missile Command. The only American missiles with real engines are the PRM's."

"PRM's?" she echoed, looking at her husband. Both were high in the Party, neither had heard of a PRM.

"Public Relations Missiles. Once in a while we fire one for effect. . . ."

"And you have four hundred cameras taking pictures," said Ivan. "You put those on television not for Americans, but for Soviets!"

"Of course," I said. "Haven't you ever wondered why all the missile pictures on our newscasts look like the same rocket? They *are* the same rocket!"

Tatiana looked at her husband, who I swear had not the smallest smile, and burst out laughing.

"If the KGB is tuned in," I said, "and they're picking up only the Russian half of this conversation, what will they think?

"And if CIA is tuned in, listening to American half?" asked Ivan.

"If CIA is tuned in," I said, "our goose is cooked! They'll call us traitors, giving away the American Prime Secret: we're not going to bomb you, we're going to run you broke buying rocket-parts!"

"If our government finds out. . . ." said Tatiana.

". . . it doesn't have to build any missiles at all," said Leslie. "You can sit here unarmed. We can't attack because our missiles have sawdust for engines. Oh, we could ship them to Moscow by registered mail, set them off with dog-whistles, but what's the use. . . ."

". . . we're wiped out six days later by our own radiation," I said. "Bomb you, and we lose *Monday Night Football*! Listen, you two, the first rule of capitalism is Create Consumers. Do you think for a minute we'd *waste precious consumers*, lose revenues from the cosmetics industry, from the *advertising industry*, for God's sake?"

He sighed, looked at Tatiana. She nodded a tiny nod.

"USSR has its own secrets," said Ivan. "To win arms race, we need America to underestimate us, to overlook change. America must think ideology is more important to Soviet Union than economy."

"You're building submarines," I said, "aircraft carriers. Your missiles have engines that work."

"Of course. But has CIA noticed our new submarines carry no missiles and have *glass windows*?" He paused, looked again to his wife. "Shall we tell them?"

She nodded a firm yes.

"There's profit in submarines. . . ," he began.

". . . *deep-water sightseeing!*" she added. "First country to put tourists on ocean floor will be rich!"

"You think we make aircraft carriers?" he asked. "Think again. Not aircraft carriers: floating condos! For people who love to travel but hate to leave home. Smog-free cities with the world's biggest tennis courts, cruise anywhere you want to live. Warm climate, maybe.

"Space program," he said. "Do you know how many people wait in line to go into space, a two-hour ride, any price we ask? It will be a hot day in Siberia," he said, smug as a cat, "when Soviet Union goes bankrupt!"

It was my turn to be astonished. "You're going to *sell space rides?* What about Communism?"

"So?" He shrugged. "Communists like money, too."

Leslie turned to me. "What did I tell you?"

"What did she tell you?" asked Ivan.

"That you're the same as us," I said, "and we should go and see for ourselves."

"For a lot of Americans," said Leslie, "the cold war stopped with a television show about the Soviets conquering the United States and replacing our government with yours. By the time the show was over, our whole country was near-dead from boredom, unable to believe that anybody could be as dull as that. We had to see for ourselves, so tourism to the Soviet Union tripled overnight."

"We are not so boring?" said Tatiana.

"Not *that* boring," I said. "Some of the Soviet system is truly dull, but some American politics would put a turkey in trance, too. What's left on both sides is not so bad. Each of us chooses what's most important to us. You sacrifice freedom for security, we sacrifice security for freedom. You don't have pornography, we don't have laws against travel. But nobody's so boring that it's time to call an end to the world!"

"In any conflict," said Leslie, "we can defend ourselves, or we can learn. Defense has made the world unlivable. What would happen if we chose to learn instead? Instead of saying *you frighten me*, what if we said *you interest me?*"

"We think our world is very slowly turning to give that a try," I said.

What had we come to learn from them, I wondered. Them is Us? Americans are Soviets are Chinese are Africans are Arabs are Asians are Scandinavians are Indians? Different expressions of the same spirit sprung from different choices, different turns on the infinite pattern of life in spacetime?

Our evening raced past midnight as we talked about what we liked and what we didn't like about the two superpowers that had such a grip on our lives. We sat close together, old friends, feeling we had loved these two all our lives.

What a difference it made to know them! After this night, we'd no more choose to launch a war on Tatiana and Ivan Kirilov than we'd fire-bomb ourselves. When they changed from Evil Empire cutouts into living human equals, into people trying as hard as we were to make sense of the world, whatever fear of them we might have had vanished. For the four of us, the treadmill had stopped.

"In Soviet Union, we have story about wolf and dancing rabbit," said Ivan, rising to act out the fable for us.

"*Shhh!*" said Tatiana, hands up for quiet. "Listen!"

He looked at her, startled.

The dark outside had begun to moan, deep and slow, as if the whole city were in pain.

Sirens were groaning, hundreds of them winding into decibels shrieking, rattling the windows.

Tatiana jumped to her feet, eyes big as dinnerplates. "Vanya!" she cried, "*Americans!*"

We ran to the windows. Lights flashed on everywhere in the city. "This can't be real!" said Leslie.

"It *is* real!" said Ivan. He turned to us, spread his hands in helpless anguish. Then he raced to a closet, pulled out two overnight bags, handed one to his wife. She scooped Petrouchka from the sofa, stuffed her barely awake into one of the bags, and they ran out, leaving the door open behind them.

A moment later Ivan reappeared, looking at us in disbelief. "What are you waiting?" he shouted. "We have five minutes! Come!"

The four of us ran down two flights of stairs into bedlam in the streets, a mass of terrified people crushing toward subways. Parents with babies in their arms, children clutching at their coats to keep up, old people struggling to move with the crowd. Some were terrified and pushing, screaming, others went quietly, knowing it was useless.

As the crowd swarmed through us, Ivan noticed, held Tatiana, moved out of the desperate river. He was breathless.

"You—you Richard and Leslie," he said, fighting tears, no anger, no hatred toward us. "You are only ones who can get away." He stopped to catch his breath, shook his head. "You don't come with us. You go . . . back the way you came." He nodded, managed a broken smile. "You go back to your world and tell them. Tell them what this is! Don't let this happen to you. . . ."

Then they were swept away in the crowd.

Leslie and I stood helpless despair on that street in Moscow, watching the nightmare come true, not caring if we got away, not caring if we lived or died. Why tell our world, I thought. It's not that your world didn't know, Ivan, but that it knew and killed itself anyway. Would our world be different?

Then the city thundered, shuddered, melted away into water flying past the seaplane's windshield. For a long time after takeoff Leslie kept her hand on the throttle, and for a long time nobody said a word.

hy?" I cried. "What is so damn wonderful about mass murder that nobody in the history of the world has ever found any smarter solution to problems than killing everybody who doesn't agree? Is that the limit of human intelligence? We're still Neanderthal? *Zog scared, Zog kill!* Is that. . . . I cannot believe that everybody has always been that . . . *stupid!* That no one has ever. . . ."

Frustration can't finish sentences. I looked at Leslie, at the tears in her eyes, down her face. What brought me to massive rage had taken her to massive sorrow. "Tatiana. . . ." she said, as broken as though we had waited for the bombs. "Ivan. . . . What sweet, funny, dear. . . . And Petrouchka. . . . Oh, God!" She burst into sobs.

I took the controls, held her hand. How I wished Pye were here! What would she say to our fury and our tears?

Damn it, I thought, for all the beauty we can be, for all the glory that so many already are, does it have to come down to the lowest clod in the world punching some button and calling an end to light? Is there nobody in the pattern who has ever come up with something better than. . . .

Did I hear it, or imagine?

Turn left. Fly till the pattern turns amber beneath you.

Leslie didn't ask why we turned or where we were headed. Her eyes were closed, and yet the tears fell.

I squeezed her hand, woke her from despair. "Hang on, little darling," I said. "I think we're going to see what a world without war looks like."

It wasn't far. I pulled the throttle back, the keel touched the water, the world turned to spray and. . . .

We came out inverted, it must have been six thousand feet in the air, then the airplane pointed straight down.

For the flash of a second I thought that the Seabird had spun out of control, then knew this was not Growly screaming down with us, it was a full-throttle fighter plane.

The cockpit was small; if Leslie and I weren't ghosts we couldn't have fit as we did, side-by-side behind the pilot.

Straight ahead of us, that is, straight *down* five hundred feet, another fighter twisted through the air, desperate to escape. The view through our windscreen chilled me cold: a circle of diamonds nearly spanned the other airplane's wings, the bright dot of our gunsight hunted for its cockpit.

World without war? After what had happened in Moscow, we were about to watch somebody get blown to pieces midair!

Half of me shrank in horror, half of me watched dispassionately. This is no jet airplane, the second half noticed, this is no Mustang or Spitfire or Messerschmitt, this is no airplane that ever existed. The fighter pilot in me observed too, approved. Good flying, I thought. Tracking the target smoothly down to firing range, pulling up as the target pulls up, rolling as the target rolls, plummeting with it once more.

Leslie was rigid beside me, breathing stopped, eyes riveted on the airplane below, the earth screaming up toward us. I put my arm around her, held her tightly.

If I could have grabbed the control stick and swerved the airplane, if I could have yanked the throttle back, I would have. There was too much noise in the cockpit to yell to a pilot intent on his kill.

On the wings of the airplane in our gunsight were the red stars of the People's Republic of China. Oh, God, I thought, has the madness spread to every world there is? Are we at war with China, too?

The Chinese plane looked for all the world like an aerobatic showplane, painted light blue beneath, greens and browns above. And despite the noise and action, our airspeed indicator showed only three hundred miles per hour. If this is war, I thought, where are the jets? What year is this?

The target snapped inverted, pulled so hard to get away that vapor trails streamed from its wingtips. Our pilot snapped too, refused to be thrown off. We didn't feel the G-forces on him, but we saw his body crush under the stress, saw his helmet sag toward the floor.

It's me, I thought. I'm a pilot again. Goddamn military! How many times do I have to make the same mistake? Here I'm about to kill somebody and I'll regret it for the rest of my life. . . .

The target rolled hard right, then, desperate, reversed its turn. At nearly point-blank range it fell directly into our gunsight's center of diamonds and the alternate me squeezed the trigger on the control stick. Machine guns fired, muffled firecrackers in the wings, and at once a puff of white smoke burst from the engine cowling of the airplane ahead.

Two words from our pilot. "Gotcha!" she said. "Almost. . . ." The voice was Leslie's! It wasn't an alternate me flying this machine, it was an alternate Leslie!

On the gunsight, a message flashed: *TARGET DAMAGED.*

"Damn!" said the pilot. "Come on, Linda. . . ."

She powered even closer to the crippled target, held the trigger down for a long burst. We smelled gunpowder in the cockpit.

Now white smoke turned to black, oil from her victim's engine flew back to streak her own windscreen.

147

TARGET DESTROYED.

"*That's* got it! *That's* got it!" said the pilot.

We heard the radio, barely. "Delta Leader, break right! Now! *Now! Break right!*"

The pilot didn't turn her head to see the danger, she slammed the control stick right, pulled as though her life depended on it. Too late.

At once our windscreen went black in hot engine oil, smoke burst from under the engine cowling, the engine stuttered, stopped, the propeller stood still.

A bell sounded in the cockpit, like the bell at round's end in a prize-fight. *SHOT DOWN* said the message in the gun-sight.

All at once it turned quiet, only the harsh cry of wind outside, the ragged burn of smoke from the engine.

I craned to look behind us, looked over our river of black into the roar of an engine overrunning us from behind, an airplane twin to the target we had just dispatched, but painted checkerboard orange and yellow. In its cockpit, as it passed not fifty feet away, the man who had just shot us laughed and waved, gleeful.

Our pilot slid her helmet visor up, waved back. "Oh, damn it, Xiao," she muttered, "I'll get you for this!"

The other blurred on by, rows of victory marks below his canopy, glossy paints flashing. Then the nose of his airplane jerked upward, a tight climbing turn to meet our wingperson screaming down on him, wild for revenge. In half a minute both airplanes, rolling half-circles around each other, were out of sight.

There were no flames in our cockpit, barely a wisp of smoke now, and for someone who had just lost a battle, our pilot was calm as scorched toast.

"Say, Delta Leader," came a voice on the radio, loud in the quiet. "Your camera's out! I've got a light here you're shot down. Tell me no!"

"Sorry, coach," said the pilot. "Win some, lose some, damn it! That was Xiao Xien Ping got me."

"Excuses, excuses. Tell it to your fans. I had two hundred dollars said Linda Albright's coming back a triple ace today and it's gone! Where you landing?"

"Shanghai Three's closest. Could make Two if you want."

"Three's fine. I'll schedule you for a reset from Shanghai Three tomorrow. Give me a call tonight, will you?"

"OK." She sounded miserable. "I'm sorry, coach."

The voice softened. "Can't win 'em all."

It was a pretty sky, a few puffs of summer cumulus, and we had plenty of altitude to glide to the airport. Even with the engine dead and oil over the glass ahead, it would not be a difficult landing. She touched a radio selector switch.

"Shanghai Three," Linda said to her microphone, "United States Delta Leader, ten south at five. Shot down to land, please."

The control tower had been waiting for her call. "U.S. Delta

Leader, you are cleared number two to land in the engine-out pattern, runway two eight right. Welcome to Shanghai. . . ."

"Thank you." She sighed, slumped in her seat.

I dared speak to her at last. "Hi," I said. "Would you mind telling us what's going on?"

I would have been startled right out of the airplane if I were her, but Linda Albright didn't seem shocked by me or my question. She answered in anger, not caring who had asked.

"I just lost us a day," she said bitterly, pounding the console with her fist. "I'm supposed to be this superstar hotrock and I just lost us ten points in the International Semifinals! Wingperson I don't care, nobody else I don't care, I will never. . . . *I will look look look look behind me!*" She exhaled deeply, then suddenly listened to her words, snapped her head to look behind her—at us. *"Who are you?"*

We told her, and by the time she had glided to the high key position for landing, she had accepted what we said, as though folks from parallel universes dropped in every few days to visit. Her mind was still on those ten points.

"It's a sport here?" I asked. "You've turned air combat into a *motor-sport?*"

"That's what they call it," she told us grimly. "AirGames. But it's no game, it is *big* business! Soon as you're out of the airpatch leagues, practically, you're worldwide telesat professional big time. I shot him down in the Singles last year, shot down Xiao Xien Ping in twenty-six minutes, but damn! I just let the man eat me up because I didn't look around, and I

150

am *yesterday's news!*" She slammed the landing gear lever down as though that could change what had happened.

"Wheels are down and locked," she said, smoldering.

It's a wingman's job to look around in combat, but her wingman had called too late. The Chinese fighter had come straight out of the sun, wide open, picked her off in one pass.

We glided down final approach to the right runway. Our wheels chirped smoothly on the concrete, we coasted to a stop on a red line just off the taxiway, television cameras craning their necks, staring.

It wasn't an airport around us as much as it was an enormous stadium, immense grandstands towering on both sides of twin runways. There must have been two hundred thousand people in the stands, ten giant daylight screens held the close-up of our fighter landing.

Yards away on the red line were two other American fighters and the Chinese that Linda had shot down. Like ours, each aircraft was sooted black, oil-drenched from mid-engine to tail. Crews were at work on the other planes, wiping them clean, replacing smoke and oil dispensers. The others, however, did not have strings of victory marks painted under the pilot's name on the cockpit.

Press and camera-crews rushed toward us for interviews.

"I hate this part," the pilot told us. "All over the world this minute, Prime War Channel's saying Linda Albright got herself redlined, shot down from behind like some first-time goddamned rookie." She sighed. "Oh, well. Grace under pressure, Linda."

In a moment the little airplane was centered close-up, a mosquito under microscopes. On the huge screens was the pilot's image at the moment she opened the canopy and took her helmet off, shook her long dark hair, pushed it back from her face. She looked chagrined, disgusted with herself. There was no image of us.

The stadium announcer reached her first. "American Ace Linda Albright!" he said to his microphone. "Victor in the most excellent battle with Li Sheng Tan, but unfortunate victim of Szechwan's own Xiao Xien Ping! Can you tell us about your battles today, Ms. Albright?"

Opposite the red line was a crowd of AirGame fans, most of them in hats and jackets with home-team fighter squadron patches, most of them Chinese. They savored the moment, watching the infield video monitors and catching glimpses between the cameras of Linda Albright in person. How welcome she was, celebrity-prize of the day! Under her image on the screen was LINDA ALBRIGHT, UNITED STATES #2, a row of 9.8's and 9.9's. The audience hushed as she spoke.

"The honorable Xiao is among the most gallant players to grace the heavens of the world," she said, the words translated through loudspeakers as she spoke. "My hand is open in respect for your great pilot's courage and skill! The United States of America will be deeply honored should one so humble as I win the chance to face him again in the skies of your beautiful country."

The crowd went wild. There was more to being an AirGames star than knowing when to pull a trigger.

The announcer touched his earphone, nodded quickly. "Thank you, Ms. Albright," he said. "We are grateful for your visit to Stadium Three, we hope that you will enjoy your visit to our city, and we wish you the best of fortunes as these International Games continue!" He turned to the camera. "We go now to Yuan Ch'ing Chih airborne in zone-four, where a major battle is shaping up. . . ."

The screens cut to an aerial view, three Chinese fighters wheeling in formation to intercept eight Americans. There was a massive gasp from the stadium; all eyes turned to the action as it began. The three were either supremely confident or they were desperate for points and glory, but the sight of courage was magnetic.

The battle was beamed from cameras on every fighter as well as from network cameraplanes; the television director must have had twenty images to choose from. And more on the way. Howling up from the runway lifted two flights of four Chinese fighters, climbing topspeed to reach the battle, to tilt the odds before the zone four clash became sports history.

Linda Albright unsnapped her shoulder harness and climbed down from her airplane, all flash and style in a fire-color silk flight suit tight as a dancer's leotard, blue satin jacket with white stars, red-and-white-striped scarf.

We waited as the interviewers crowded for just-down-from-the-sky footage with her. Pilot training must have taught her as much tact and courtesy as aerobatics and gunnery. For every question she had an unexpected answer, modest and confident at once. By the time she had finished, there was a crowd pressing her with its own questions, programs in Chinese with her full-page photograph to sign.

153

"If this is what it's like when she loses in a foreign country," said Leslie, "what happens when she wins back home?"

In time the police wedged a path to a limousine and half an hour later we were together in quiet. The airport stadium was framed in one set of the penthouse hotel-suite windows, the city and the river in another. It was a city like the Shanghai of our own time but even bigger, taller and more modern. AirGames replays and commentary chattered from the television screen.

Linda Albright touched a control console to turn it off, collapsed on the sofa. "What a day!"

"How did it happen?" asked Leslie. "What made you. . . ."

"I broke my own rule," said her alternate self. "*Always look behind!* Xiao's a marvelous pilot, we could have had a terrific battle, but. . . ."

"No," said my wife, "I meant how did the Games happen? And why? What do they mean?"

"You *are* from another time, aren't you?" said the pilot. "Some utopia where there's no competition, is it, some world without war? Dull as dirt."

"We're not from a world without war," I said, "and it isn't dull, it's stupid. Thousands of people die, millions. Our politics scare us, our religions pit us against each other. . . ."

Linda fluffed a pillow behind her head. "Thousands of us die, too," she said in disgust. "How many times do you think I've been killed in my career? Not too many since I turned professional, knock wood, but days like today do happen. In 1980, the entire American Air Team was shot down three days in a row! Without air cover for three days, you can imagine what happened to us in Land and Sea! The Poles. . . . Well," she threw up her hands, shook her head, "they couldn't be stopped, they wiped us out of world competition. Three divisions, three hundred thousand players! Redlined the entire American team. Zero!"

The retelling eased her anger at her own loss today.

"Not that we weren't in good company," she said. "They annihilated the Soviet Union, they wiped out Japan, Israel. When they finally beat Canada for the Gold, you can imagine. Poland went wild, the whole country just went crazy. They bought their own channel for the celebration!"

Remembering, she seemed almost proud.

"You don't understand," said Leslie. "Our wars aren't games. We don't just kill players on scorecards. In our wars, people really die!"

The sparkle faded. "They do in ours, too, sometimes," Linda said. "AirGames have midair collisions. The British lost a SeaGames ship and its whole crew in a storm last year. But LandGames are the worst, that's fast machinery in rough country. A little more courage than sense when they get on camera, if you ask me. Too many accidents. . . ."

"Do you know what Leslie's saying?" I asked her. "In real life, for us, things get deadly serious."

"Look," she said, "as long as you're trying to accomplish something, things will get dangerous and deadly serious! We've got the Mars station now with the Soviets, we've got the Alpha Centauri mission coming up next year, practically every scientist in the world is in on that one. But a multi-trillion-dollar industry's not going to stop because of some accidents."

"There's no way to get through to you, is there?" said Leslie. "We're not talking about accidents, we're not talking about games or competition. We're talking about deliberate, premeditated, wholesale murder."

Linda Albright sat up, looked at us amazed. "My God!" she said suddenly. "You mean *war!*" It had been so unthinkable she had never considered it.

She was suddenly sympathetic, concerned. "Oh, I'm sorry!" she said. "I never imagined. . . . We had wars, too, years ago. World wars, till we knew the next one would be the end of us."

"What did you do? How did you stop?"

"We didn't stop," she said. "We changed."

She smiled, remembering. "The Japanese started it all, selling cars. Thirty years ago, Matsumoto got into air-racing in America—a publicity stunt, they put the Sundai automobile engine into a raceplane. They mounted microcameras in the wings for the National Air Races, shot some good footage and turned it into the first Sundai Drive commercials. Nobody cared that they finished fourth, Sundai sales went out of sight."

"That changed the world?"

"Slow-motion, it did. Along came Gordon Bremer, the airshow promoter, got the idea to put TV microcams and lasertally guns in showplanes, laid down the rules, offered big prizes for air combat pilots. It was a local show for a month or so, then all of a sudden air combat was a spectator sport like nothing you've ever seen. It's team play with stars, it's all the strategy of karate and chess and fencing and football in three dimensions, fast and loud and it looks more dangerous than hell."

Her eyes sparkled again. Whatever had called Linda Albright to the sport still held her. No wonder she was good at it.

"Those cameras put the fans right in the cockpits, there was nothing like it! Every week it was the Kentucky Derby, the Indianapolis Five Hundred and the Super Bowl in one. When Bremer syndicated the show nationwide, he might as well have put a match to guncotton. Right away it was the second-biggest television sport in America, then it was the first-biggest, then the American AirGames hit telesat all over the world. Wildfire!"

"Money," said Leslie.

"You'd better believe, money! Cities bought franchises for AirGames fighter teams, then there were national teams from the playoffs. Then — and here's where things really changed — international competition, a sort of professional Air Olympics. Two billion television sets tuned for seven days while every country that could get planes in the air fought like crazy. Can you imagine the ad revenues, with an audience that size? Some countries paid their national debts with the income from that first competition."

We listened, spellbound.

"You can't believe how fast it happened. Every town with an airport and a few planes sponsored its amateur team. Cities

. . . in a few years slum kids were sports heroes. If you thought you were fast and smart and brave, if you didn't mind being an international television star, you could earn more money than Presidents can dream of.

"Meanwhile, the Air Forces were being aced out. As soon as their tours were up, pilots quit and joined the Games. Of course, no one would enlist. Who wants to be an underpaid officer living under military law on some godforsaken air base, logging time in simulators that are more exams and stress than flight, flying airplanes that are more big and deadly than fun, when the only sure bet is you're first to get killed when there's a war? Not too many!"

Of course, I thought. Had there been civilian flying teams when I was a kid, a chance to earn a place in thundering speed and glory somewhere other than the military, young Richard would no more have joined the Air Force than he would have volunteered for prison.

"But, with all that money, why are you flying propeller planes?" I said. "You've got, what is it, six hundred horsepower? Why no jets?"

"Nine hundred horsepower," said the pilot. "Jets were too dull. They had closing speeds twice as fast as sound. A short battle lasted half a second, a long battle might have lasted thirty seconds, and most of that time the planes were out of sight. Blink and you miss the action. After the novelty wore off, viewers tired of the jets. It's not easy to root for some university technician flying a supersonic computer with wings."

"I can see what would attract pilots," said Leslie. "But what about armies and navies?"

"They weren't far behind. The armies had so many tanks in Europe they thought why not put some cameras on them and cash in on all that iron? And of course the navies weren't going to be left out. They got into it in a big way; two weeks of SeaGames that first year — the America's Cup with laser-guns.

"They called it the Third World War Games, but the military was slow and dull. On television you don't win with drones who can't think for themselves and machines that don't work, you win by scoring hits.

"Then private industry came in with civilian teams for Land and Sea, lighter and faster and smarter. The military was embarrassed out of the Games. Couldn't keep soldiers or tankdrivers or ship commanders when the money and the glory was in non-military combat teams."

Lights blinked on her telephone. She ignored them, caught up in the fun of telling these two from a war-planet about the Games.

"No one thought about fighting for real anymore, there was so much planning and training for the Games. No point plotting a war that might come true in some would-be future when there's instant gratification fighting right now and making money at it!"

"Did the military go out of business?" I asked, joking.

"In a way, they had to. Governments funded armies out of habit for a few years but the tax revolt and other protests stopped that."

"And the military died?" I asked. "Thank God!"

"Oh, no," Linda laughed. "The people rescued it."

"The people *what?*" said Leslie.

"Oh, don't get me wrong," said Linda. "We love the military! I check their little block on my tax form and give them a fortune every year. Because they changed! First they learned to lighten up, got rid of their corruption and bureaucracy, and they quit spending tons of money on junk. They saw their only chance for funding was to do something the Games couldn't do, and do it well. Dangerous, exciting work, work that required the resources of nations: *colonies in space!* Ten years later we had the Mars station working, and now we're on the way to Alpha Centauri."

It could work, I thought. Never had I thought there could be any alternate to war but total peace. I was wrong.

"This could work!" I told Leslie.

"It does work," she said. "It's working here."

"Work!" said Linda. "That's another thing—what it did for the economy. There was a monster demand for excellence in the Games. Mechanics, technicians, pilots, strategists, planners, support groups. . . . The money is unbelievable. I don't know what management gets, but a good player can earn millions. Between base pay, victory bonuses and discovery bonuses for every new kid we find and train . . . well, we earn more money than we know how to spend. There's enough danger to keep us happy—a little more than enough, sometimes. Opening round especially, you don't want to doze off, there's forty-eight fighters all clawing into one video-block. . . ."

There was a soft chime from the door.

"There's enough press for the world's biggest egos, like mine," she said, moving to answer. "And of course nobody has to guess who might win the next war, they just wait till June twenty-first and catch it on telesat. Lots of folks bet on favorites, of course. Makes you feel like a racehorse, sometimes. Excuse me a minute." She opened the door.

The man was hidden behind a giant spray of spring flowers. "Poor darling," came his voice, "do we need sympathy tonight?"

"Krys!" She threw her arms around him, the doorway framing two figures in brilliant flight suits, butterflies in flowers. I looked to Leslie, asked silently if it wasn't time for us to be on our way. Her alternate self would be hard pressed to continue a chat with people her friend couldn't see. But when I turned back to the doorway, I knew we wouldn't be having that problem. The man was me.

"Sweetheart, what are you doing *here*?" asked Linda. "You should be in Taipei, you're flying third period Taipei!"

The man shrugged and looked at his flying boot, scuffed it on the carpet. "But it was grand battle, Lindie!" he said.

Her mouth fell open. "You were *shot down?*"

"Damaged only. Your United States squadron leader is incredible pilot." He paused, savoring her astonishment, burst into laughter. "But not that incredible. He forgets white smoke is not black smoke. My last-ditch, I put wheels down, flaps down, full throttle snap over the top of the turn, and there he is in my sight and I *get him!* Luck, but director said it is beautiful on screen. Twenty-two-minute fight! By then Taipei is out of range, so I call Shanghai Three. Not till I land do I see your airplane parked, black as sheep! Soon as my interviews are done, I think my wife needs a little cheer-up. . . ."

At that moment, he glanced across the room, saw us, turned back to Linda. "Ah! The press. I'm sorry. Shall I leave you for a while?"

"Not the press," she said, watching his face. Then to us, "Richard and Leslie, this in my husband, Krzysztof Sobieski, the Number One Polish Ace. . . ."

The man was not quite so tall as I, his hair was lighter than mine, his eyebrows heavier, his jacket crimson and white, emblazoned *Squadron One—Air Combat Team of Poland.* Aside from that, I might as well have been watching my own startled reflection. We said hello, while Linda explained us as simply as she could.

"I see," he said, uneasy but accepting us because his wife had. "Your place, where you come from, it is much like ours?"

"No," I said. "Seems to us as if you've built your world around games. As if your planet's a fun house, some kind of carnival. It's a little bizarre to us."

"You just told me your world is built around war, *real war,* deliberate, premeditated mass murder, a planet bent on self-destruction," said Linda. "Now *that's* bizarre!"

"This seems like fun house to you," her husband rushed to explain, "but here is peace, lots of work, prosperity. Even

162

arms industry is booming, but airplanes and ships and tanks come now with blank-guns and flame-kits and laser-talleys. Why fight, why kill ourselves for nothing, when we can put same fight on telesat and live to spend royalties? Makes no sense to kill ourselves for one battle. Do actors kill themselves for one movie? Games are big industry. Some people say gambling on Games is bad, but better we gamble, we think, than . . . how do I say . . . disintegrate ourselves?"

He ushered his wife to the couch, held her hand as he talked. "And Lindie is not telling what relief it is not to hate anybody! Today I see my wife is shot down by Chinese pilot. Do I go crazy mad, I hate the man who shot her, I hate Chinese, I hate living? Only thing I hate is to be in this poor man's boots next time my Lindie finds him in the air. She is Number Two American Ace!" He looked into her frown. "She does not tell you, I guess?"

"I'll be Number Last if I don't look around," she said. "I've never felt so dumb, Krys, I've never felt so . . . first thing I know, there's the shotdown light and floof! the engine quits! And there goes Xiao tearing by, laughing his head off. . . ."

The lights that at first had flashed occasionally on the telephone console grew more insistent. Finally the phones rang through, a deluge of priority calls: producers, directors, team officials, city officials, press and television requests, urgent invitations. Had these two lived in our time we'd have thought they were rock stars on tour.

So much to ask, I thought, but not only did they have to plan tomorrow's strategy with their support teams, they had to talk with each other, and sleep.

We rose while they were both on the phone, waved them a silent goodbye. Linda covered her speaker with her hand.

"Don't go! We'll be just a bit. . . ."

Krys covered his phone, too. "Wait! We can have dinner! You please stay!"

"Thank you no," said Leslie. "You've given us too much time already."

"Happy landings, you two," I said. "And Ms. Albright, from now on, let's look behind us, OK?"

Linda Albright covered her face in mock shame, blushing, and their world disappeared.

$\mathcal{B}$ack in the air again, we chatted on excited about Linda and Krys and their time, a grand alternative to the constant war and preparing-for-war that locked our own world in its high-tech Dark Age.

"Hope!" I said.

"What a contrast!" said Leslie. "Makes you see just how much we're squandering on fear and suspicion and war!"

"How many other worlds down there are as creative as theirs?" I said. "Are there more like them or more like us?"

"Maybe they're *all* creative here! Let's land!"

∞

The sun overhead was a sphere of soft copper fire in a violet sky. Twice as large as the sun we knew but not so bright, closer but no warmer, it bathed the scene in gentle gold. The air smelled ever so faintly of vanilla.

We stood on a hillside where forest met meadow, a spiral galaxy of tiny silver flowers shining around us. Away below on one hand lay an ocean nearly as dark as the sky, a diamond river shimmering toward it. On the other, as far as we could see, stretched a broad plain to horizons of pristine hills and valleys. Deserted and still, Eden revisited.

First glance, I would have sworn we were marooned on an earth untouched by civilization. Had people turned to flowers?

"This is . . . it looks like *Star Trek,*" said Leslie.

Alien sky, lovely alien earth. "Not a soul," I said. "What are we doing on a wilderness planet?"

"It can't be wilderness. We've got to be here somewhere."

Second glance said look again. Under the distant landscape lay the faintest of checkerboards, subtle dark lines in city blocks, broad straights and angles as if there had been highways once for traffic long ago rusted into air.

My intuition rarely fails. "I know what happened. We've found Los Angeles, but we're a thousand years late! See? That's where Santa Monica used to be, Beverly Hills over there? Civilization's gone!"

"Maybe," she said. "But Los Angeles never had this sky, did it? Or two moons?" She pointed.

Way off over the mountains, sure enough, floated a red moon and a yellow one, each smaller than earth's moon would ever be, one rising ahead of the other.

"Hm," I said, convinced. "Not Los Angeles. *Star Trek.*"

A movement in the woods opposite.

"Look!"

The leopard came toward us from the trees, its coat the color of sunset brass marked in bold snowflakes. I thought leopard for its markings, though the beast was the size of a tiger. It moved at an odd halting pace, struggling uphill, and we heard it panting as it approached.

There's no chance it can see us, or attack, I told myself. It doesn't look hungry, though with tigers that's hard to tell.

"Richie, it's hurt!"

That queer pace wasn't because this was an alien creature but because some terrible force had crushed the animal. Golden eyes ablaze with pain, it lurched heavily as if its life depended upon dragging itself across the clearing and into the forest behind us.

We ran to help, though I didn't know what we could have done even were we solid flesh.

Up close it was huge. As tall as Leslie at its shoulder, the giant cat must have weighed a ton.

We could hear agony in its breathing, knew it didn't have

long to live. Blood was caked and nearly dry on its shoulders and flanks. The animal collapsed, rallied for a few steps, collapsed again among the silver flowers. In the last minutes of its life, I thought, why is it so desperate to reach those trees?

"Richie, what can we do? We can't just stand here helpless!" There was anguish in her eyes. "There has to be a way. . . ."

Leslie knelt by the massive head, reached to soothe the broken animal, comfort it, but her hand passed through its fur, nor could the creature feel her touch.

"It's all right, sweet," I said. "Tigers choose destinies same as we do, dying's no more the end of life for them than it is for us. . . ." True, I thought, but what cold comfort.

"No! We couldn't have come here to see this beautiful . . . to watch it die? Richie, *no!*"

The giant quivered, in the grass.

"Dear one," I said, drawing her up to me, "there's a reason. There's always a reason. We just don't know what it is right now."

The voice from the edge of the forest was as loving as sunlight, but it carried like a thunderbolt across the meadow.

"Tyeen!"

We whirled to look.

At the edge of the flowers stood a woman. I thought at first it was Pye, but her skin was lighter, her maple hair longer than our guide's. Still she was as much a sister to our other-world self as she was to my wife, the same curve of cheek, the same square jaw. She wore a dress of spring green, over it a cloak of dark emerald that reached to the grass.

As we watched, she ran toward the broken animal.

The great creature stirred, lifted its head, coughed a last broken roar across the flowers to her.

The woman reached it in a swirl of greens, knelt beside it unafraid, touched it gently, her hands tiny on the enormous face. "Up, now. . . ." she whispered.

It struggled to obey, paws kicking air.

"I'm afraid it's badly hurt, ma'am," I said. "There's probably not too much you can do. . . ."

She didn't hear. Eyes closed, she brought herself into loving focus on the monster form, stroked it lightly. Then suddenly she opened her eyes and spoke. "Tyeen. Little one, rise up!"

With another roar, the tiger sprang to its feet in a spray of flying grass, breathing deep, towering over the woman in the flowers.

She stood and put her arm up around the animal's neck, touched its wounds, smoothed the fur on its shoulders.

"Silly cat, Tyeen," she said. "Where is your knowing? This is not your time to die!"

The matted blood was gone, dust brushed from the exotic coat. The great creature looked down to this person, closed its eyes for a moment, nuzzled her shoulder.

"I'd ask you to stay," said the woman, "but tell that to hungry cubs, hm? Go on. On your way."

A growl like a dragon's, reluctant to leave.

"Go! And careful on the cliffs, Tyeen," she said. "You're not a mountain goat!"

The giant swung its head toward her, then shook itself and loped away, easy grace across the meadow, rippling shadows and gone in the trees.

The woman watched till it was out of sight, turned to us, matter-of-fact. "Loves heights," she said, resigned to folly. "Thrilled with heights, and she can't understand that every rock won't take her weight."

"What did you do?" said Leslie. "We thought . . . it looked so bad, we thought. . . ."

The woman turned and walked toward the hilltop, motioning us to join her. "Animals heal quickly," she said, "but sometimes they need a little love to help them through. Tyeen's an old friend."

"We must be old friends, too," I said, "since you can see us. Who are you?"

She studied us as we walked, that stunning face, eyes deeper green than her cloak, scanning each of us laser-fast for a moment, tiny left-right sweeps, speed-reading our souls. The intelligence in those eyes! No pretense, no protections.

Then she smiled, as if something all at once made sense.

"Leslie and Richard!" she said. "I'm Mashara!"

How could she know us? Where had we met? What did she mean to this place, and what did the place mean to her? My questions blurred. What kind of civilization lives out there invisible? What are its values? *Who is this person?*

"I am you in my dimension," she said as if she'd heard my thoughts. "Those who know you here call you Mashara."

"What is this dimension?" said Leslie. "Where is this place? When . . . ?"

She laughed. "I have questions for you, too. Come."

Just beyond the edge of the meadow was a house no larger than a mountain cabin. It was built of rock without mortar, the stones shaped and set so that the edge of a playing card could not have slipped between them. There was no glass in the windows; likewise there was no door.

A family of plump ground-birds trotted single-file through the yard. A fluffy creature curled on a tree branch, all ringtail fur and bandit-mask, opened its eyes for a moment as we approached, closed them again to sleep.

Mashara invited us in, stepping first through the doorway. Inside, what looked like a young llama the color of a summer cloud dozed on a carpet of leaves and straw near the window, curious enough to tilt its ears toward us but not so curious to stand.

The little house had no stove or pantry or bed within, as though this person neither ate nor slept, yet it was filled with warmth and gentle safety. If I had to guess, I would have said that Mashara was the good witch of the forest.

She led us to benches at a table near the large window, her view of trees and meadow and valley spread below.

171

"Mine's a parallel spacetime from yours," said the woman, "but of course you know that. Different planet, different sun, different galaxy, different universe. Same Now."

"Mashara," said Leslie, "did something terrible happen here, a long time ago?"

I caught her thought. The lines on the earth, the planet turned to wilderness. Could Mashara be the last survivor of a civilization that once had ruled this place?

"You remember!" said our alternate self. "But is it bad for a civilization that wrecks the planet from seafloor to stratosphere . . . is it terrible for that civilization to pass away? Is it bad for a planet to heal itself?"

For the first time I felt unsettled with this place, imagining what its last days must have been, screaming whimpering death.

"Is it good for any life to perish?" I asked.

"Not to perish," she said after a moment, "but to change. There were aspects of you who chose that society. Aspects who reveled in it, aspects who worked desperately for change. Some won, some lost, all of them learned."

"But the planet recovered," said Leslie, "look at it! Rivers and trees and flowers . . . it's beautiful!"

"The planet recovered, the people didn't." She looked away.

There was no ego in this person, there was no modesty, no judgment. There was only the truth of what had happened.

The llama rose to its feet, ambled slowly out the door.

"Evolution made civilization steward of this planet. A hundred thousand years later, the steward stood before evolution not helper but destroyer, not healer but parasite. So evolution withdrew its gift, passed civilization by, rescued the planet from intelligence and handed it to love."

"This. . . ." said Leslie, "this is your job, Mashara? Rescuing planets?"

She nodded. "Rescuing this one. To the planet, I'm patience and protection, I'm compassion and understanding. I'm the highest aims the ancient people saw in themselves. A dear culture in so many ways, a gifted society, trapped at last by its greed and lack of vision. It ravaged the forests into desert, consumed the soul of the land in mine-pits and waste, smothered its air and its oceans, sterilized the earth with radiation and poisons. A million million chances it had to change, but it would not. From the ground it dug luxury for a few, jobs for the rest, and graves for the children of all. In the end, the children didn't agree, but the children had come too late."

"How could a whole civilization have been so blind?" I asked. "What you're doing now. . . . You have the answer!"

She turned to me, implacable love. "I don't have the answer, Richard," she said. "T am the answer."

It was quiet for a while. The edge of the sun touched the horizon, but it would be a long time till dark.

"What happened to the others?" asked Leslie.

"In the last years, when they saw it was too late, they built hyperconductive supercomputers, built us in their domes, taught us to restore the earth, turned us loose outdoors to work in air they could no longer breathe. Their last act, apologizing to the earth, was to give us the domes to save what wildlife we could. Planetary reconstructive ecologists, they called us. They named us, they blessed us, then they went out together into the poison where the forests used to be." She looked down. "And they were gone."

We listened to the echo of her words, imagined the loneliness and desolation this woman must have endured.

She had dropped the phrase so lightly. "Mashara," I said, "they *built* you? You're a *computer?*"

The lovely face turned to me. "I can be described as a computer," she said. "So can you."

Part of me knew, as I asked, that I was losing the big picture, losing who she was in what she was.

"Are you. . . ." I said. "Mashara, are you alive?"

"Do you find that impossible?" she asked. "Does it make a difference whether humanity shines through carbon atoms or silicon or gallium? Is there anything that's born human?"

"Of course! The lowest . . . even destroyers, even murderers are human," I said. "We may not like them, but they're human beings."

She shook her head no. "A human being is an expression of life, bringing light, reflecting love across whatever dimension it chooses to touch, in whatever form it chooses to take. Humanity isn't a physical description, Richard, it's a spiritual goal. It's not something we're given, it's something we earn."

A stunning thought, to me, forged in the tragedy of this place. No matter how I tried to see Mashara as a machine, a computer, an *it*, I couldn't. It was not the chemistry of her body that defined her life but the depth of her love.

"I guess I'm used to calling people human," I said.

"Maybe you should re-think," she said.

A freak-show part of me goggled at the woman through the haze of her new label. A supercomputer! I had to test her. "What's thirteen thousand two hundred ninety seven divided by two point three two three seven nine zero zero one squared?"

"Must you know?"

I nodded.

She sighed. "Two four six two point four zero seven four zero two five eight four eight two eight zero six three nine eight one. . . . How many decimal places would you like?"

"Amazing!" I said.

"How do you know I'm not making it up?" she said mildly.

"I'm sorry. It's just, you seem so. . . ."

"Want a final test?" she said.

"Richard," said Leslie, a voice in caution.

The woman glanced thanks to my wife. "Do you know the final test of life, Richard?"

"Well, no. There's always a line between. . . ."

"Answer one question for me?"

"Of course."

She looked directly into my eyes, the good witch of the forest, unafraid of what had to come.

"Tell me," she said, "how would you feel if I died, this moment?"

Leslie gasped.

I leaped to my feet. "No!"

A stab of panic knifed through me, that the highest love our alternate self would pick might be to self-destruct, to let us feel the loss of the life she was. "Mashara, *no!*"

She fell as lightly as a flower and lay unmoving, still as death, lovely green eyes gone lifeless.

Leslie rushed to her, ghost of person to ghost of computer, to hold her as gently as the good witch had held the great cat she loved.

"And how will you feel, Mashara," Leslie said, "when Tyeen and her cubs and the forests and seas and the planet you were given to love die with you? Will you honor their lives as we honor yours?"

Ever so slowly, life returned, the lovely Mashara stirred, moved to face her sister from another time. Mirrors of each other, the same proud values shining in different worlds.

"I love you," said Mashara slowly sitting, turning to look at us. "You must never think . . . that I can't care. . . ."

Leslie smiled, the saddest smile. "How can we look at your

planet and think you can't care? How can we love our own earth without loving you, dear steward?"

"You must go," Mashara said, her eyes closed. Then a whisper, "Please remember?"

I took my wife's hand, nodded.

"The first new flowers we plant every year, the first new trees," said Leslie, "we plant for Mashara."

The llama stepped softly through the doorway, ears forward, eyes dark, velvet nose extended in concern to the woman who meant home. The last we saw, the good witch of the forest had put her arms around its neck, warm reassurance.

The little house melted into spray and sunlight, Growly pulling free again above the pattern.

"What a lovely soul," I said. "One of the dearest human beings we've ever known is a computer!"

e flew wrapped in Mashara's love, still flooded with images of her beautiful planet. How right it seemed to have friends in worlds other than our own!

Some of our exploration had been joy, some had been horror, but our learning curves were going straight up, we'd seen things, felt things we couldn't have imagined if we'd lived a hundred lifetimes.

We wanted to go on.

Nearby, the pattern turned soft rose, the paths glowed golden below. I didn't need intuition to know that I wanted to touch those colors. I looked to Leslie. She nodded.

"Ready for anything?"

"I think so. . . ." She gave me her terrified-passenger impression, arms braced against the glareshield.

When we came out of the spray of the landing, we hadn't moved from the cockpit—we found ourselves idling gently across the water. This was no ocean, and the pattern was gone.

We floated on a mountain lake, pines and firs down to honey-color beach, water glittering clear beneath us, sunlight rippling on sand. We drifted for a moment, trying to understand.

"Leslie!" I said. "This is where I practice water landings, this is Lake Healey! We're out of the pattern!"

She looked for any sign to tell her otherwise. "Are you sure?"

"Pretty sure." I checked again. Steep slopes of forest on the left, low trees at the end of the lake. Beyond the trees would be the valley floor.

"Hurray!" I said, but the word felt hollow, and I said it alone.

I turned to Leslie.

Her face was etched in disappointment. "Oh, I know I should be glad, but we were just beginning to learn, there was still so much to understand!"

She was right. I felt cheated, too, as though the lights had come up, the actors quit and walked offstage before the play was over.

I lowered the water rudder, pressed the pedal to turn toward the beach, heard Leslie catch her breath.

"Look!" She pointed.

Just forward of the right wingtip as we turned, nose drawn up on the sand, was a Martin Seabird.

"Aha!" I said. "This is it, I'm sure. Everyone practices here. We're home, all right."

I touched the throttle and we whispered across the lake toward the other seaplane.

There was no movement anywhere, no sign of life. I shut the engine down and we coasted silent the last few yards. The bow scraped gently on the sand two hundred feet from the other machine.

I slipped off my shoes, stepped into ankle-deep water, helped Leslie from the plane. Then I lifted the bow of the flying boat and slid it another foot farther onshore.

Leslie walked to the other Seabird while I set our anchor in the sand.

"Hello?" she called. "*Hello!*"

"Nobody home?" I said, walking to join her.

She didn't answer. She was standing by the other airplane, looking into its cockpit.

The flying-boat was Growly's twin, painted in the snow-and-rainbow design we had created ourselves. The interior of the cabin was the same color, it had the same fabric, the same carpet on the floor—it was our design down to the custom glareshield and lettering on the instrument panel.

"Coincidence?" Leslie asked. "Another seaplane *exactly like Growly?*"

"Odd. Very odd."

I reached to touch the cowling. The engine was still warm.

"Uh-oh," I said, an eerie feeling coming over me. I took Leslie's hand and we walked back toward our own airplane.

Midway she stopped, turned back. "Look at that! Not a footprint, except ours. How can someone land, get out of their airplane, disappear and not leave one footprint?"

We stood between the two Growlys, baffled. "Are you sure we're home?" she asked. "It feels like we're still in the pattern."

"A duplicate Lake Healey?" I asked. "And how can *we* leave footprints if we're still ghosts?"

"You're right. And if we'd landed in the pattern, we'd have found some aspect of us," she said. She stood wordless for a moment, looked back toward the other Seabird, puzzled.

"If we're still in the pattern, it could be a test," I said. "Since nobody seems to be here, the lesson might be that they are, in some other form. We can't be separated from ourselves. We're never alone unless we believe we are."

A strobe of ruby laser flashed twenty feet away and there in white jeans and blouse stood our Indian alter-self.

181

"Why do I love you? Because you *remember!*" She held her arms out to us.

"Pye!" My wife ran to hug her.

In this place, pattern or not, we weren't ghosts, and hug they did.

"It's so good to see you!" said Leslie. "You can't imagine where we've been! The dearest, and the most wicked . . . oh, Pye, there's so much to tell you, so much we need to know!"

Pye turned to me.

"We're glad you're back!" I said hugging her, too. "Why did you leave so suddenly?"

She smiled, walked to the edge of the water and sat cross-legged on the beach, patted the sand for us to join her.

"Because I was pretty sure what was going to happen," she said. "When you love someone, when you know they're ready to learn and grow, you set them free. How could you learn, how could you feel your experiences if you knew I was there, a shield between you and your choices?"

She turned to me, smiling. "This *is* an alternate Lake Healey," she said. "The seaplane is for fun. You reminded me how much I love to fly, so I twinned your Growly, took off to practice, and to find you. A surprise, isn't it, landing wheels-down in the water?"

She saw my horror, held up a hand. "Caught it in time. A moment before I touched, I called on the skill of the aspect of me most current in seaplanes, and you yelled *wheels up!* Thank you."

She touched Leslie's shoulder. "How observant you are to notice I left no footprints in the sand. That was to remind you to choose your own path, follow your highest sense of right, and not someone else's. But you already know that."

"Oh, Pye," said Leslie, "how can we follow our highest sense of right, what can we do in a world that. . . . Did you know Ivan and Tatiana?"

She nodded.

"We loved them!" said Leslie, her voice breaking. "And it was *Americans* who killed them! Pye, it was *us!*"

"It was not you, dear one. How could you think you would kill them?" She lifted Leslie's chin, looked into her eyes. "Remember, nothing in the pattern is random, nothing is without a reason."

"What possible reason?" I snapped. "You weren't there, you didn't feel the terror!" The night in Moscow came flooding back, as though we had murdered our own family in the dark.

"Richard, the pattern holds all possibilities," she said gently, "absolute freedom of choice. It's like a book. Every event is a word, a sentence, part of an endless story; every letter stays forever on the page. It is *consciousness* that changes, choosing what to read and what to leave unread. When you turn to a page about nuclear war do you despair, or do you learn what it has to tell? Will you die reading the page, or will you move on to other pages, wiser for what you've read?"

"We didn't die," I said. "And I hope we're wiser."

"You shared one page with Tatiana and Ivan Kirilov, and at

the end of your reading that page was turned. It still exists, this moment, waiting to change the heart of anyone who chooses to read it. But after you've learned, you don't have to read it again. You've moved past that page, and so have they."

"They have?" said Leslie daring to hope.

Pye smiled. "Didn't Linda Albright remind you just a little of Tatiana Kirilova? Didn't Krzysztof remind you in the smallest way of your friend Ivan? Have your AirGames pilots not changed war from terror into entertainment, and saved their world from destruction? *Who do you think they are?*"

"The same ones," said Leslie, "who read that page with us about a terrible night in Moscow?"

"Yes!" said Pye.

"And they're us, too?" I asked.

"Yes!" Her eyes sparkled. "You and Leslie, Linda and Tatiana and Mashara and Jean-Paul and Attila and Ivan and Atkin and Tink and Pye, we *all* — are — one!"

Tiny waves lapped on the sand, and we could hear the wind soft in the trees.

"There is a reason I found you," she said, "a reason you found Attila. You care about peace and war? You land on pages that give you insight into peace and war. You fear that you'll be separated, or that you'll die and lose each other? You land in lifetimes that will teach you about separation and death, and what you learn will change the world around you ever after. You love the earth and worry that humankind is destroying it? You see the worst and the best that can happen, and you learn that all depends on your own individual choice."

"Are you telling us that we create our own reality?" I asked. "I know it's a saying, Pye, but I don't agree. . . ."

She laughed merrily, then pointed to the horizon in the east.

"It is early, early morning," she said, her voice suddenly low and mysterious. "Dark. We stand on a beach like this beach. First hint of dawn. Cold."

We were there in the cold and dark with her, living her story.

"In front of us stands our easel and canvas, we hold our paints and brushes." It felt like being hypnotized, those dark eyes. I felt the palette in my left hand, the brushes in my right, brushes with rough wooden handles.

"Now the light rises in the sky, do you see it?" she said. "The sky is turning to fire, gold pouring, ice prisms melting into sunrise. . . ."

We saw, stunned in colors.

"Paint!" said Pye. "Catch that sunrise on your canvas! Take the light of it on your face, through your eyes, spread it into art! Swiftly now, swiftly! Live the dawn with your brush!"

I'm no artist, but in my mind was that glory, turned to bold slashes on canvas. I imagined Leslie's easel, saw her own dawn wonderfully delicate there, careful beams blended to a starburst in oils.

"Done?" said Pye. "Brushes up?"

We nodded.

"What have you created?"

I should have painted our teacher, that moment, she was so darkly bright.

"Two very different sunrises," said Leslie.

"Not two sunrises," said Pye. "The artist does not create the sunrise, she creates. . . ."

"Oh, of course!" said Leslie. "The artist creates the *painting!*"

Pye nodded.

"The sunrise is reality, the painting is what we make of it?" I asked.

"Exactly!" said Pye. "If each of us had to create our own reality, can you imagine the chaos? Reality would be limited to whatever each of us could invent!"

I nodded and imagined. How to create a sunrise if I'd never seen one? What to do with a black night sky to start the day? Would I have thought of a sky? Of night and day?

Pye went on. "Reality has nothing to do with appearances, with our narrow way of seeing. Reality is love expressed, pure perfect love, unbrushed by space and time.

"Have you ever felt so at one with the world, with the universe, with *everything that is*, that you were overcome with love?" She looked from Leslie to me. "*That* is reality. *That* is the truth. What we make of it is up to us, as the painting of the sunrise is up to the artist. In your world, humanity has strayed from that love. It lives hatred and power-struggles and manipulations of the earth itself for its own narrow reasons. Continue and no one will see the sunrise. The sunrise will always exist, of course, but people on earth will know nothing of it and finally even stories of its beauty will fade from their knowing."

Oh, Mashara, I thought. Must your past be our future?

"How can we bring love to our world?" asked Leslie. "There are so many threats, so many . . . Attilas!"

Pye stopped for a moment, searching for a story to tell us, then drew a little square in the sand.

"Let's say we live in a terrible place: Threat City," she said, touching the square. "The longer we stay there, the less we like it. There's violence, destruction, we don't like the people, we don't like their choices, we don't belong there. Threat City is not our home!"

She drew a wavy line away from the square, angles and switchbacks. At the end of the line, she drew a circle.

"So one day we pack our bag and drive away, seeking the town of Peace." She traced the difficult road she had made, followed all its twists and turns with her finger. "We choose left turns and rights, highways and shortcuts, we follow the map of our highest hopes and at last here we are, rolling into this gentle little place."

Peace was the circle in the sand, and Pye's finger stopped there. As she spoke, she planted tiny evergreen twigs in the sand for trees.

"We find a home in Peace, and as we get to know the people, we discover that they share the same values that brought *us* there. Each has found her own road, has followed his own map to this place where the people have chosen love and joy and kindness—to each other and to the town and to the earth. We didn't have to convince everyone in Threat City to move to Peace with us, we didn't have to convince anyone but ourselves. Peace already exists, and anyone who wishes can move there whenever they choose."

She looked to us, almost shy with her story.

"The people of Peace have learned that hatred is love without the facts. Why tell lies to separate and destroy ourselves when the truth is we're one? The people of Threat City are free to choose destruction, and we're free to choose peace.

"In time, other people in Threat City may grow tired of violence, perhaps they'll follow their own map to Peace, make the same choice that we made to leave destruction behind. If they all make that choice, Threat City will become a ghost town."

She traced a figure eight in the sand, a smooth curving road between Peace and Threat City.

"And one day the people of Peace, remembering, curious, might visit the ruins of Threat City to find that with the destroyers gone, reality is visible again: fresh streams instead of running poisons, new forests springing up from clearcuts and strip mines, birds singing in clean air." Pye planted other twigs in the new town. "And the people of Peace take down the sign hanging crooked at the edge, the sign that says Threat City, and they put up a new sign: Welcome to Love. And some move back to clear the rubble, rebuild the mean streets gentle, and they promise the town will live by its name. Choices, my dear ones, do you see? It's all choices!"

That moment, in that odd place, what she said made sense.

"What can you do?" she asked. "In most worlds sudden miracles aren't the way things change. Change comes with the spinning of one trembling fragile strand between countries: the first amateur AirGames in Linda Albright's world, the first Soviet dancers or singers or films that play to American audiences in yours. Slowly, slowly, keep choosing life."

"Why not overnight?" I said. "There's nothing that says quick change is impossible. . . ."

"Of course quick change is possible, Richard," she said. "Change happens every second, whether you notice it or not. Your world, with its first strand of hope for a future in peace, is just as true as your alternate world that ended in 1962 on the first day of its last war. Each of us chooses the destiny of our world. Minds must change before events."

"Then it's true, what I told the lieutenant!" I said. "One of my futures in 1962 was that the Soviets didn't back down. And I began a nuclear war."

"Of course. The pattern has thousands of paths that come to an end that year, thousands of alternate Richards who chose death-experiences there. You didn't."

"Now wait," I said. "In the alternate worlds that didn't survive, weren't there innocent people just riding along when they blew up, or were frozen or vaporized or eaten by ants or whatever?"

"Certainly. But Richard, the destruction of their planet is

189

what they chose! Some chose by default: they didn't care; some because they believed in defense-become-attack; some because they thought they were powerless to stop it. One way to pick a future is to believe it's inevitable."

She paused, tapped the circle with its tiny trees. "When we choose peace, we live in peace."

"Is there a way to talk with the people who live there, a way to talk with an alternate us when we need to know what they've learned?" asked Leslie.

Pye smiled at her. "You're doing that now."

"But how do we do it," I said, "without hopping into a seaplane and finding a trillion-to-one chance into a different dimension to meet you?"

"You want some way to talk with any alternate self you can imagine?"

"Please," I said.

"It's not very mysterious," she said, "but it works. Imagine the self you want to talk with, Richard, make believe you ask whatever you need to know. Pretend you hear the answer. Try it."

I was suddenly nervous. "Me? Now?"

"Why not?"

"Do I close my eyes?"

"If you want."

"No ritual, I suppose?"

"If ritual makes you comfortable," she said. "Take a deep breath, imagine a door opening into a room filled with many-colored light, see the person moving in the light, or in a mist. Or forget the lights and mist, and pretend you hear a voice; sometimes we hear sounds better than we visualize. Or forget light and sound, just feel that person's knowing flood into your own. Or forget intuition and imagine that the next person you meet will give you the answer if you ask, and ask. Or say a word that has magic for you. As you wish, imagine."

I chose imagination, and a word. Eyes closed, I imagined that when I spoke, I'd find in front of me an alternate self to tell me what I needed to know.

Relaxing, I saw soft colors, floating pastels. When I say the word I will see this person, I thought. There is no hurry.

Colors drifted, clouds behind my eyes.

"One," I said.

In a shutter-flash I could see: the man stood by the wing of an old biplane parked in the hay, blue sky and a flare of sun behind him. I couldn't see his face, but the scene was quiet as Iowa summer, and I heard his voice as though he sat with us on the beach.

"Before too long, you'll need all your knowing to be able to deny appearances," he said. "Remember, that to get from one world to the next in your interdimensional seaplane, you need Leslie's power, she needs your wings. Together you fly."

The shutter flashed again, startled my eyes open.

"Anything?" said Leslie.

"Yes!" I said. "But I'm not quite sure how to use it." I told her what I'd seen and heard. "I don't understand."

"You'll understand when you need to," said Pye. "When you find learning before experience, it doesn't always make sense right away."

Leslie smiled. "Not everything we learn here is practical."

Pye retraced the figure eight in the sand, thinking. "Nothing's practical until we understand it," she said. "There are some aspects of yourselves that would worship you for God because you fly a Martin Seabird. There are others you could meet you'd swear were magic themselves."

"Like you," I said.

"Like any magician," she said, "I seem magic because you don't know how I've been practicing! I'm a point of consciousness expressing itself in the pattern, just as you do. Like you, I was never born and I can never die. Even separating *me* from *you*, remember, implies a difference that's not there.

"As you're one with the person you were a second ago or a week ago," Pye continued, "as you're one with the person you're going to be a moment from now or a week from now, so you're one with the person you were a lifetime ago, the one you are in an alternate lifetime, the one you'll be a hundred lifetimes into what you call your future."

She stood, dusted the sand from her hands.

"I must be on my way," she said. "Don't forget the artists

and the sunrise. No matter what happens, no matter what appears to be, the only reality is love."

She reached to Leslie, hugged her goodbye.

"Oh Pye!" said Leslie. "How we hate to see you go!"

"Go? I can disappear, little ones, but I can never leave you! How many of us are there, after all?"

"One, dear Pye," I said, hugging her farewell.

She laughed. "Why do I love you?" she asked. "Because you remember. . . ."

And she vanished.

Leslie and I sat on the beach for a long time near Pye's drawing in the sand, tracing the figure eight she had drawn, loving her little towns and forests and the story she had told.

At last we walked to Growly, arms around each other. I coiled the anchor line, helped Leslie into the cockpit, pushed the seaplane away from the shore and climbed aboard. The Martin weathervaned slowly into the breeze, and I started the engine.

"I wonder what's next," I said.

"It's strange," said Leslie. "When we landed here and thought we were out of the pattern, I was sad to think it was over! Now I feel. . . . Seeing Pye again completed something for me. We've learned so much so fast! I wish we could go home and think about it, sort out what it means. . . ."

"Me, too!" I said.

193

We looked at each other for a long moment, agreed without a word.

"OK," I said, "home it is. The next thing we have to learn is how."

I reached to the throttle and pushed it forward. No imagining, no struggle to visualize. Growly's engine roared and the seaplane surged ahead. Why, I thought, should this simple act be so difficult when I can't see the throttle?

The instant Growly lifted from the water, the mountain lake vanished and we were aloft again over every possible world that can be.

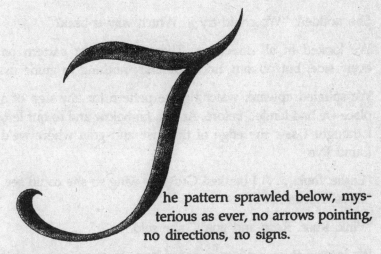

he pattern sprawled below, mysterious as ever, no arrows pointing, no directions, no signs.

"Any ideas? How do we begin?" I asked.

"Follow intuition, the same as always?" asked Leslie.

"Intuition is too general, too full of surprises," I said. "We didn't go looking for Tink or Mashara—or Attila. Can intuition take us to the exact place in the pattern where we were on our way to Los Angeles?"

It felt like one of those wicked intelligence tests, easy when you know the answer but by the time you find it you've been driven insane.

Leslie touched my arm. "Richard, when we first landed in the pattern," she said, "we didn't find Attila or Tink or Mashara. At first we could recognize ourselves: in Carmel when we met, then the young you and me? But the farther we flew. . . ."

"Right! The farther we flew, the more we changed. So you're saying let's head back, see if anything looks familiar? Of course!"

She nodded. "We could try it. Which way is back?"

We looked in all directions. There was bright pattern on every side, but no sun, no landmarks; nothing to guide us.

We spiraled upward, watching the pattern for any sign of a place we had landed before. At last, far below and to our left, I thought I saw the edge of the rose-and-gold where we'd found Pye.

"Leslie, look. . . ." I banked Growly's wing so she could see. "Does it seem. . . ."

"Pink. Rose. Rose and gold!" she said.

We looked at each other, guarded hope in our eyes, spiraled higher.

"That's it," said Leslie. "And way out there . . . beyond the rose, is that green? Where we found Mashara?"

We banked hard left, heading toward the first familiar sights we'd seen in the pattern.

The seaplane droned on over the matrix of lifetimes, a tiny mote in that vast sky, past Mashara's greens and golds, past the corals hiding that heartbreaking night in Moscow, past

Attila's burgundy darkness. It felt as if we'd been flying hours since takeoff.

"When Los Angeles first disappeared, the water was blue with paths of gold and silver, remember?" said Leslie, pointing to the distant horizon. "Is that it? *Yes!*" Her eyes sparkled with relief. "This isn't so hard. Is this so hard?"

Yes, it is, I thought.

As we crossed the edge of blues and golds, they spread before us to the end of sight. Somewhere out there was a precise few feet of water where we needed to touch down, the doorway to our own time. Where?

We flew on, turning this way and that, watching for the two bright paths that had taken us to our first meeting in Carmel. There were millions of paths below, millions of parallels and intersections.

"Oh, Richie," said my wife at last, her voice as heavy now as it had been light before. "We'll never find it!"

"Of course we will," I said. But my inner self was afraid she was right. "Time to try intuition again? We don't have much choice. It all looks the same down there."

"OK," she said. "You or me?"

"You," I said.

She relaxed in her seat, closed her eyes, and went quiet for a few moments.

"Left turn." Could she hear the sorrow in her voice? "Bring it way around to the left and down. . . ."

∞

The tavern was nearly deserted. There was one man alone at the end of the bar, a white-haired couple in a booth at the side.

What are we doing in a *barroom*, I thought. I've hated them my life long, I cross streets to avoid them. "Let's get out of here."

Leslie put a hand on my arm, stopped me from leaving. "A lot of places felt like mistakes when we landed," she said. "Was Tink a mistake? Was Lake Healey?"

She walked toward the bar, turned to look at the old couple in the booth, and her eyes widened.

I joined her. "Amazing!" I whispered. "It's us, all right, but. . . ." I shook my head.

But *changed*. Her face was as lined as his, her mouth as hard. He was drawn, the color of ash. Not old: beaten. On the table stood two bottles of beer, hamburgers and french-fries on plates. Face down between them was a paperback copy of our last book. They were deep in conversation.

"What do you make of that?" Leslie asked, hushed too.

"An alternate us, in our own time, reading our book in a bar?"

"Why don't they see us?" she asked.

"They're probably drunk," I said. "Let's go."

She ignored that. "We should talk to them, but I hate to

barge in, they seem so grim. Let's sit in the next booth for a minute and listen."

"Listen? You want to *eavesdrop*, Leslie?"

"No?" she asked. "OK, then you go barge in and I'll join you as soon as I see they want company."

I studied the two. "Maybe you're right," I said.

We slipped into the booth next to them, sat on the far side so we could watch their faces.

The man coughed, tapped ,the book in front of his wife. "I could've done it!" he said between bites of his hamburger. "Could've done everything in this book!"

She sighed. "Maybe you could have, Dave."

"Well, I could!" He coughed again. "Look, Lorraine, the guy flies an old biplane. So what? I started flying, you know that. Nearly soloed. What's so hard about flying an old plane?"

I didn't write that it was hard, I thought. I wrote that I was barnstorming when I realized my life wasn't going anywhere.

"There are other things in the book besides old planes," she said.

"Well, he's a damn liar. Nobody makes a living that way, selling rides from some hayfield. That's made up. His fancy wife, she's probably made up, too. None of it's true. Can't you see that?"

Why was he so cynical? If I read a book by an alternate me, wouldn't I see myself on the pages? And if he's an aspect of who I am now, I thought, why don't we have the same values? What's he doing in a bar drinking *beer*, for God's sake, eating the ground-up burned-up body of some poor dead cow?

He was an unhappy soul this day, and from the look of things he'd been that way a long time. His was the face I saw in the mirror every day, except the lines there were so sharp and deep it looked as if he'd been trying to cross his face out with a knife. There was a pinched feeling about him, a tightness in the air and I wanted to get away from him, get out of there.

Leslie saw my distress, reached to me, held my hand for patience.

"So what if they're both made up, Davey?" asked the woman. "It's just a book. What makes you so mad?"

He finished his hamburger, reached a french-fry from her plate. "All I'm saying is that you bugged me and bugged me to read it and I did. I read it, and there's nothing so damn special in it. I could have done everything this guy did. I don't see why you think it's so . . . whatever you think it is."

"I don't think it's whatever. I think it's what you just said, I think it could have been us in that book."

When he looked at her startled, she raised her hand let me talk.

"If you had gone on with your flying, who knows? And you were writing, too, remember, working at the *Courier* and writing stories at night? Just like him."

"Fff!" he said. "Stories at night. And what came of them?

Rejections. A box of printed little rejection slips, not even full size paper. Who needs it?"

Her voice was almost gentle. "Maybe you quit too soon."

"Maybe so. I tell you I damn well could have written that seagull thing he wrote! I used to go out on the jetty when I was a kid, watch the birds fly. Wished it was me with wings. . . ."

I know, I thought. You'd wedge yourself down in those great boulders, crouch out of sight, and the gulls would fly so close you could hear! the wind on their wings, feathery swords hurling past. Then a turn and flash and they'd be off downwind, going like bats, free in the sky and there you sat, anchored in solid rock.

Suddenly I was swept with compassion for the man, felt my eyes stinging as I watched that worn face.

"I could have written that book, every word." He coughed again. "I'd be a rich man today."

"Yeah," she said.

She was quiet, finished her hamburger. He ordered another beer, lit a cigarette, disappeared for a time in blue smoke.

"Why'd you quit flying, Dave," she asked, "if you wanted to do it so much?"

"I never said? Simple. You either had to pay a damn fortune to learn, like it was twenty dollars an hour back when you could live for a week on twenty dollars, or you'd work like a slave, polishing airplanes for days, pumping gas morning to night to get one flight. I've never been a slave to any man!"

She didn't answer.

"Would you do it?" he asked. "Would you come home smelling like gas and wax every night of your life for one hour's flight a week? It would've been a year to get my license at that rate." He exhaled, a long sigh. "They call you *line-boy*. 'Line-boy mop that oil.' 'Line-boy sweep the hangar.' 'Line-boy dump the trash.' Not me!"

He drew on his cigarette as though it were the memory itself smoldering.

"Army wasn't much better," he said out of the cloud, "but at least the Army paid me cash." He looked out across the room unseeing, his mind in another time. "We'd go out on maneuvers, and sometimes the fighters'd come down over us like spears glancing, you know, down and then up right out of sight, and I'd wish I'd joined the Air Force instead. I would have been a fighter pilot."

Nope, I thought. Army was your smart move, Dave. Army, you mostly kill one person at a time.

He exhaled again, and coughed. "I don't know, maybe you're right about the book. Could have been me. Sure could have been *you*. You were pretty enough to be a movie actress." He shrugged. "They do go through some bad times together in that book. Course it's his own fault." He paused, took another long drag, looking sad. "I don't envy them that, but I do sort of envy the way things turned out."

"Don't you get wistful on me," she said. "I'm glad we're not them! Their life has some nice things but it's all on the edge, it's too unknown for me. I couldn't sleep if I were her. You and me, we've had a good life—good jobs, we've never once been out of work or bankrupt and we're never going to be. We've got a nice house, some money saved. We're not the wildest people in the world, maybe we're not the happiest people, but I love you, Dave. . . ."

He grinned and tapped her hand. "I love you more than you love me. . . ."

"Oh, David!" she said, shaking her head at him.

They were quiet for a long time. How they had changed, to me, in just this little while near their table! I wished Dave had never learned to smoke, but I liked the guy. I had switched from aversion to sympathy for a side of myself I had never known. Hatred is love without the facts, Pye had said. Whoever we dislike, are there facts we could learn that would change our minds?

"You know what I'm going to get you for our anniversary?" she asked.

"Anniversary presents, is it now?" he asked.

"Flying lessons!" she said.

He looked at her as if she'd taken leave of her senses.

"You can still do it, Davey. I know you can. . . ."

They were quiet for a moment. "Damn," he said. "It's not fair."

"Nothing's fair," said his wife. "But you know, sometimes they say six months and then it just goes away, people live for years!"

"Lorraine, it went so *fast*. Yesterday, I joined the Army, that was thirty years ago! Why don't they tell you it goes so fast?"

"They do," she said.

He sighed. "Why didn't we listen?"

"Would it have made a difference?"

"It would now," he said, "if I had it to live over, knowing."

"What would you say to our children now, if we'd had any?" she asked.

"I'd tell 'em think about everything. *Do I really want to do this?* Doesn't matter what you do, matters if you *want to do it!*"

She looked at him surprised. He doesn't talk this way often, I thought.

"I'd tell 'em it's no fun," he said, "when you come down to your last six months, to wonder what happened to the best you could have been, what happened to what matters?" He coughed and frowned, stubbed his cigarette in the ashtray. "I'd tell 'em nobody means to get carried away in . . . mediocrity, but it happens, kids, it happens unless you think about everything you do, unless you make every choice the best one you know how to make."

"You should have written, Davey."

He waved his hand no. "It's like, at the end, there's this surprise quiz: am I proud of me? I gave my *life* to become the person I am right now! Was it worth what I paid?"

All at once he sounded terribly tired.

Lorraine pulled a tissue from her purse, put her head on his shoulder and touched her tears. Her husband held her, patted her, wiped his own eyes, and the two fell silent but for his stubborn cough.

It might have been too late to tell his children, I thought, but he had told someone. He had told his wife and he had told us, a table and a universe away. Oh, Dave. . . .

How often had I imagined this man, how many times had I tested decisions on him: if I say no to this test, if I play it safe, how will it feel when I look back on what I've done? Some choices were easy no's: no I don't want to rob banks, no I don't want to addict myself, no I don't want to trade my life for a cheap thrill. But the choice to follow any real adventure was measured by the view from his eyes: when I look back on this, will I be glad I dared, or glad I didn't? Now here he was in person, telling us.

"The poor things!" Leslie said, softly. "Is that us, Richie, wishing we'd lived differently?"

"We work too hard," I murmured back. "We're so lucky to have each other. I wish we'd take more time to enjoy it, just be quiet together."

"Me, too! You know, we can slow down, wookie," she said. "We don't have to go to conferences and make films and take on ten projects at the same time. I guess we didn't even have to fight the IRS. Maybe we should have left the country, gone to New Zealand and had a vacation for the rest of our lives, like you wanted to."

"I'm glad we didn't," I said. "I'm glad we stayed." I looked at her, loved her for the years we'd had together. No matter they'd been a struggle, they'd also been the greatest joy in my life.

Hard times, beautiful times, she said with her eyes, I wouldn't trade them, either.

"Let's take a long vacation when we get back," I said, new perspective from this fading couple, new insight coursing through me.

She nodded. "Let's re-think our lives."

"You know what I think, Davey my sweet?" said Lorraine, managing a smile.

He cleared his throat, smiled back. "I never know what you think."

"I think we ought to take this napkin here," she reached into her purse, "and this pencil, and we ought to list what we want to do most and make this the best six months . . . the best time of our lives. What would we do if there were no doctors with all their do's and don'ts? They admit they can't cure you, so who are they to tell us what to do with whatever time we have left together? I think we ought to make this list and then go ahead and do what we want."

"You're a crazy girl," he said.

She wrote on the napkin. "Flying lessons, at last. . . ."

"Oh, come on," he said.

"You said it yourself, you could do what that guy did," she said, touching the book. "This is just for fun. Come on. What else?"

"Well, I've always wanted to travel, go to Europe maybe, as long as we're dreaming here."

"Where in Europe? Anyplace special?"

"Italy," he said, as though he'd dreamed it all his life.

She raised her eyebrows, wrote it down.

"And before we go, I'd like to learn a little Italian so we can talk to the people over there."

She looked up amazed, her pencil stuck in the air for a moment.

"We'll get some Italian books," she said, writing. "And I know they have it on cassettes, too." She looked up. "What else? The list is for *anything you want.*"

"Oh, we don't have time," he said. "We should have done this. . . ."

"Should have, fiddlesticks," she told him. "No sense wishing for a past we can't do anything about. Why not wish for things we still can do?"

He thought about that for a moment, and his wistful look vanished. It was as if she had breathed new life into him. "Damn right!" he said. "About time! Add surfing!"

"*Surfing?*" she said, her eyes wide.

"What's the doctor going to say to that?" he said, a devilish smile on this face.

"He'll say it's not healthy," she laughed, and wrote it down. "Next?"

Leslie and I grinned at each other.

"They may not have told us how to get home," I said, "but they sure told us what to do when we get there."

Leslie nodded, pushed the invisible throttle forward and the room tumbled away.

16

*B*ack in the air again, we searched for any clue the pattern might offer, any sign of a way to get home. The paths, of course, went every direction at once.

"I wonder," said Leslie. "Are we going to spend the rest of our days popping in and out of other people's lives looking for our own?"

"No, sweetie, it's right here," I lied. "It's got to be! We just have to be patient until we find the key, whatever it is."

She looked at me. "You're feeling a lot clearer than I am right now. Why don't you pick a spot for us to try?"

"Intuition, one last time?"

As soon as I closed my eyes, I knew this was it. "Straight ahead! Get set to land."

He was collapsed alone on the bed in a hotel room. My twin, my exact twin, propped up on one elbow, staring out the window. He wasn't me, but he was so close that I knew we couldn't be far from home.

Glass doors framed a balcony overlooking a golf course, tall evergreens beyond. Low clouds, the steady pelt of rain on the roof. It was either late afternoon or the clouds were so thick and dark that noon had turned to dusk.

Leslie and I stood on a matching balcony on the opposite side of the room, looking in.

"I get the feeling he's awfully depressed, don't you?" she whispered.

I nodded. "Strange for him to lie there doing nothing. Where's Leslie?"

She shook her head, watched him, concerned. "I feel . . . awkward in this situation," she said. "I think you should talk to him alone."

The man lay unmoving, yet he wasn't asleep.

"Go on, sweetheart," she urged, "I think he needs you."

I squeezed her hand, moved into the room without her.

He stared into the gray, barely tilted his head when I appeared. Next to him on the bedspread was a laptop computer, power-light glowing but its screen as blank as his face.

"Hi, Richard," I said. "Don't be startled. I'm. . . ."

"I know," he sighed. "The projection of a troubled mind." He turned his eyes back to the rain.

I thought of a tree, lightning-blasted, toppled here unable to move.

"What happened?" I asked.

No reply.

"Why are you so depressed?"

"It didn't work out," he said at last. "I don't know what happened." Another pause. "She left me."

"Leslie? Left you?"

A half-nod from the form on the bed. "She said if I didn't get out of the house, she would, she couldn't stand me anymore. I may be the one who flew away, but she's the one who left the marriage."

Impossible, I thought. What would it take for an alternate Leslie to say she couldn't stand him anymore? So many terrible times we had come through together, my Leslie and I, years of struggle after my bankruptcy, times we were so tired we could hardly go on, so pressured we'd lost perspective and patience, times we'd quarreled. But never was it *serious*, never did we part, never did anybody say if you don't leave I will. What could have happened to them that was so much worse than what had happened to us?

211

"She won't talk to me." His voice was as listless as his body. "Soon as I try to discuss things with her she hangs up."

"What did you do?" I said. "Did you take up drinking, drugs? Did you. . . ."

"Don't be an idiot," he said irritably. "I'm me!" He closed his eyes. "Get out of here. Leave me alone."

"I'm sorry," I said. "That was dumb of me. It's just that I can't imagine what it would take to break you two up. It had to be something monumental!"

"No!" he said. "Little things, it was all little things! There's this mountain of work—taxes and accounting and films and books and a thousand requests and offers from all over the world. It's got to be done and done *right,* according to her, so she goes at it like a crazy woman, she never stops. Years ago she promised me my life would never again be the mess it was before she met me. And she meant it."

He rambled on, glad to talk even to his mind's projection.

"I just don't care about trivia, I never did, so she takes it on herself to do it all, juggling three computers with one hand and ten hundred forms and requirements and deadlines with the other. She's going to keep that promise if it kills her, do you understand?"

He said that last as though he meant if it kills *me.* He was resentful, bitter.

"She has no time for me, no time for anything but work. And I can't help her because she's scared to death I'll mess it up again.

"So I remind her this is a world of illusions, don't take it so seriously, and I think I'll go fly the airplane for a while. Simple truth, but when I leave, she glares at me like she'd like to vaporize me!"

He lay on the bed as though it were an analyst's couch.

"She's changed, the stress has changed her. She isn't charming or funny or beautiful anymore. It's like she's driving a bulldozer on a land-fill and there's so much paper has to be moved by April fifteenth or December thirtieth or September twenty-sixth she's going to be buried in it if she doesn't keep moving, and I say what's happened to our lives and she yells well if you carried some of the load around here you might find out!"

If I didn't know he was me, I would have said the man was raving.

Yet I had nearly taken his road, once, nearly gone as crazy as he sounded. It's so easy to get lost in a typhoon of detail, to put off the most important things in life because you're sure nothing can threaten a love that special, and then discover one day that living itself has turned into a detail, and in the process you've become a stranger to the one you love most.

"I've been where you are," I said, bending truth. "Would it be all right if I asked you one question?"

"Go ahead," he said, "ask. Nothing can hurt. It's the end of us. It wasn't *my* fault. Little things can be deadly, sure, but this is *us*! Soulmates! Can you imagine? I fall back into my old ways, a little less than neat for a few days, and she complains I'm making work for her when she's already drowning. She makes a list of little things she wants me to do and I don't get to them for a while, I forget something as silly as changing a light bulb and she accuses me of making her carry all the responsibility. Do you see what I mean?

"Sure I should help out, but all the time? And even if I don't, is that enough to break up our marriage? Shouldn't be. But pebble after pebble it piles up and suddenly the whole bridge collapses. I told her to snap out of it, look at the bright side, but *noooo*! Our marriage used to be love and respect, now it's strain and endless work and anger. She just can't see what's most important! She. . . ."

"Say, guy, tell me something," I said.

He stopped complaining, looked at me, surprised I was still there.

"Why should she think you're worth it?" I asked. "What's so great about you that she ought to be in love with you?"

He frowned, opened his mouth, but no words came. I might as well have been a wizard, stole his power of speech. Then he looked away, puzzled, into the rain.

"What was the question again?" he asked after a while.

"What is there about you," I said patiently, "that your wife ought to love?"

He thought again, shrugged and gave up. "I don't know."

"Are you loving to her?" I said.

He shook his head, ever so slightly. "Not anymore," he said, "but it's difficult when. . . ."

"Are you understanding, supportive?"

"Honestly?" He thought some more. "Not really."

"Are you open, sensitive to her feelings? Are you caring, compassionate?"

"Can't say that I am." He looked grim. "No."

He considered every question I asked. I wondered if it took courage to answer, or if despair was forcing him to face the truth.

"Are you communicative, a good conversationalist — entertaining, interesting, enlightening, enthusiastic, inspiring?"

He sat up for the first time, looked at me. "Sometimes. Well, hardly ever." A long pause. "No."

"Are you romantic? Are you thoughtful? Do you do sweet little things for her?"

"No."

"Are you a good cook? Are you orderly around the house?"

"No."

"Are you reliable, a problem-solver? Are you a haven from stress for her?"

"Not really."

"An astute businessman?"

"No."

"Are you her friend?"

He thought longest about that. "No, I'm not," he said at last.

"If you'd showed up with all these faults on your first date with her, do you think she'd have wanted a second?"

"No."

"Then why hasn't she left you before this," I said, "why has she stayed?"

He looked up in pain. "Because she's *married to me?*"

"Probably so." We were both quiet, thinking about that.

"Do you think it's possible for you to change," I asked, "to turn these no's to yeses?"

He looked at me, haggard from his answers. "Of course it's possible. I used to be the best friend she had, I used to be. . . ." He paused, trying to remember what he used to be.

"Would these things, would these qualities hurt you if you had them back?" I asked. "Would practicing them . . . *diminish* you, somehow?"

"No."

"What have you got to lose by giving them a try?"

"Nothing, I guess."

"Do you think there'd be anything for you to gain?"

"I'd have a lot to gain!" he said finally, as though the idea were brand new to him. "I think she might love me again. And if she did, we'd both be happy." He thought back. "Every moment together used to be glorious. It was romantic. And we'd explore ideas, find new insights . . . it was always exciting. If we had time, we'd be like that again."

He paused, then spoke his truest truth. "I really could help her more than I do. It's just that I've gotten so used to her doing everything, it's been easier to let her do it. But if I helped, if I did my part, I think I'd get back my self-respect."

He got up, looked in the mirror, shook his head, began pacing about the room.

The transformation was remarkable. Does he really understand just like that, I wondered.

"Why couldn't I have figured it out for myself?" he asked. He glanced at me. "Well, in fact, I guess I did."

"It took years to slip down to where you are," I said, a voice of caution, "how many years to climb back up?"

The question startled him. "None," he said. "I just changed! I can't wait to try this!"

"That fast?"

"It doesn't take time to change once you understand the problem," he said, his face lit with excitement. "Somebody hands you a rattlesnake, it doesn't take long to drop it, does it? I should hold on to this snake because it's me? No thanks!"

"A lot of people would."

He sat in the chair by the window, looked at me. "I'm not a lot of people," he said. "I've been lying here the last two days thinking that the loving souls Leslie and I used to be had slipped off into a different happy future together and left us in this miserable dimension where we can't even talk.

"I was so sure it was her fault I couldn't see a way out,

because to make things better *she* had to change. But now. . . . If it's *my* fault, I can change it! If I change and stay changed for a month, and we're still unhappy, *then* we can talk about changing her!"

He was up, pacing again, looking at me as though I were a brilliant therapist. "You know, just a few questions! Why did I need you to walk in from wherever you walked in from? Why didn't I ask those questions? Months ago!"

"Why didn't you?" I asked.

"I don't know. I got so buried in resenting her and all the problems . . . it's like she was *causing* them instead of trying to deal with them, and I was feeling sorry for myself, thinking how different she was from the woman I'd loved so much."

He sat back on the bed, put his head in his hands for a moment. "You know what I was thinking when you came in here? What's the last act of a desperate man. . . ."

He walked to the balcony, looked out at the view as if it were sunshine instead of rain. "The answer is to *change*. If I can't change my own mind, I deserve to lose her! But now that I see, I know how to make her happy. And when she's happy. . . ." He stopped and looked at me, grinning. "Well, you have no idea!"

"Why should she believe you're transformed?" I asked. "It's not every day you walk out of the house uncaring and come back the loving guy she married."

He thought about that, sad again for a moment. "You're right," he said. "There's no reason for her to believe it. It may take her days to know it, or months, or never. She may never want to see me again." He thought a moment more, turned to me. "The truth is that my changing's up to me. Whether she notices—how she feels about it, is up to her."

"If she won't listen to you," I said, "how are you going to tell her what's happened?"

"I don't know," he said softly. "I'll have to find a way. Maybe she'll hear it in my voice."

He walked to the telephone, dialed a number.

It was as if I had already disappeared, so intent was he on this call, so filled with a future he had nearly lost.

"Hi, sweetheart," he said. "I understand if you want to hang up, but I've learned something you might like to know."

He listened, his mind become eyes on a wife a hundred miles away.

"No, I called to tell you you're *right*," he said, "*I'm* the problem. I've been wrong, and selfish, and unfair to you and I can't begin to tell you how sorry I am! I'm the one who has to change, and I already have!"

He listened some more. "Sweetie, I love you with all my heart. More than ever now that I understand how much you've gone through to stay with me this long. And I swear, I'm going to make you glad that you did!"

He listened again, smiled the smallest of smiles. "Thank you. In that case, I wonder if you'd have time . . . for one date with your husband, before you never see him again?"

17

I left as he talked, slipped out to the balcony to my Leslie, kissed her softly. We held each other, glad to be together, glad to be us.

"Will they stay together?" I asked. "Can anybody make so many changes so fast?"

"I hope so," said Leslie. "I believe him because he didn't defend himself. He wanted to change!"

"I always imagined that soulmates have an unconditional love, that nothing can tear them apart."

"Unconditional?" she said. "If I'm cruel and hateful for no reason, if I stomp all over you, will you love me forever? If I beat you senseless, I'm gone for days, I'm in bed with every man on the street, I gamble away our last cent and come home drunk, will you cherish me anyway?"

"When you put it that way, my love could flicker," I said. The more we're threatened, I thought, the less we love. "Interesting, to love someone unconditionally is *not to care* who they are or what they do! Unconditional love comes out the same as indifference!"

She nodded. "I think so, too."

"Then love me conditionally, please," I said. "Love me when I'm the best person I can be, cool off if I go thoughtless and boring."

She laughed. "I will. You do the same, please."

We peeked into the room once more, saw the other Richard still on the phone and smiled.

"Why don't you try the takeoff this time," said Leslie. "You really should know you can do it before we go home."

I looked at her, reached in that moment of clarity for the throttle of our invisible seaplane, visualized it under my hand, pushed it forward.

Nothing. No rippling of hotel or mountains or trees, no flickering of the world about us.

"Oh, Richie," she said, "it's easy. Just focus up."

Before I could try again there came that familiar quaking rumble, the universe blurring into its time-shift. She had already pushed the lever forward.

"Let me try again," I said.

221

"OK, sweetie," she said. "I'll pull it back. Remember, the trick is *focus. . . ."*

In that instant we broke free into the air, the sea beneath us. As she brought the throttle back, the engine backfired, started to recover, too late.

The Martin pitched up, then down into the water.

I knew it would be a hard landing. What I didn't expect was the crash, as violent as a bomb exploding up in the cockpit.

A monster force snapped my seat belt like string, hurled me through the windshield, face down in highspeed water. When I fought up, gasping, there was the Seabird fifty feet away, tail to the sky, steam roiling up as the hot engine slid under.

No! I thought. *No! NO!* I dove after the plane, our beautiful white Growly gone murky underwater, dove to the shattered cockpit as it sank. Pressure in my ears, broken structure groaning around me, I tore what was left of the canopy away, unstrapped Leslie's body, limp, unresisting, her white blouse floating ethereal slow-motion about her, golden hair graceful languid free, pulled her loose and started up, the surface dim, so high above us. She's dead. No, no, no. Let me die now, let my lungs break, let me drown!

A lie drove me on: you're not sure she's dead. You've got to try.

She's dead.

You've got to try!

One chance in a thousand. By the time I reached the top I

was utterly totally exhausted. "It's OK, sweet," I panted. "We're going to make it. . . ."

A fishing boat, big twin outboard motors, almost ran us over, sliding huge broadside from top speed, smothering us in foam, a man hurling down through the spray, trailing a lifeline.

In the water no more than ten seconds, he yelled, "Got 'em both! Haul!"

I was no ghost and this was no dream. This was real stone, ice-hard on the side of my cheek. I was not standing dispassionate to watch some scene, I *was* the scene, no one else to watch.

I lay on her grave, on the hillside she had planted with wildflowers, and sobbed. Cold grass beneath me. On the stone against my face, one word: *Leslie.*

Autumn wind, I didn't feel it. Home in my own time, I didn't care. Utterly and completely alone three months after the crash, I was still dazed. It felt as if a hundred-foot stage curtain laced with weights had fallen on me, smothering me, tangling me, trapping me in loss and musty grief. I had never realized what courage it takes when a wife dies, when a husband dies, not to kill ourselves. More courage than I had. It took every promise I had made to Leslie.

How many times we had made our plans: die together, whatever happens, we'll die together. "But in case we don't," she had warned me, "if I die first, you must stay on! Promise!"

"I'll promise if you promise. . . ."

"No! If you die, there's no point in my living anymore. I want to be with you."

"Leslie, how do you expect me to promise to live on if you won't promise, too? That's not fair! I'll promise because there's a chance it could happen for a *reason*. But I'm not going to promise unless you do."

"A reason? What possible reason?"

"It's theoretical, but maybe you and I could find some way to get past it. If love isn't the motivation to overcome death, I don't know what is. Maybe we'd learn how to be together no matter that we were taught to believe that death is the end of us. Maybe it's just a different perspective, an hypnosis, and we could de-hypnotize ourselves. What a gift it would be to write that!"

She had laughed at me. "You little sweetie, I love the way your mind works away at these things," she said. "But you're making my point, don't you see? Not only are you the one who reads death-books, you're a writer. So if there's a chance to do this . . . de-hypnotizing, there's a point to your staying if I die. You could learn and you could write about it. But there's no point in my staying if you die. I wouldn't write without you. So promise!"

"Listen to this," I'd tell her, reading from a death-book:

"'. . . and as I stood alone in our parlor, grieving desperately for my dear Robert, a book fell from the shelf, entirely unbidden. I jumped, for it startled me so, and when I lifted it from the floor, the pages fell open and my finger touched the sentence, *I am with you!* underlined in his own pen.'"

"That's very nice," she had said. My wife the skeptic had taken our discussions on this subject with many a grain of salt.

"Do you doubt this?" I had asked her. "Are you a doubting Leslie?"

"Richard, I am telling you, if you die. . . ."

"What would people think?" I had told her. "We run around saying, we run around *writing*, for God's sake, that the challenge of life in spacetime is to use the power of love to turn disaster into glory and one minute after I'm dead you pick up your Winchester and shoot yourself?"

"I don't think I'd care what people thought at a time like. . . ."

"You don't think you'd care! *Leslie Maria* . . . !"

And so we had talked, round and round. Neither could bear the thought of life without the other, but each had promised at last, exhausted, there would be no suicide.

Now I regretted every word. Secretly I had known that if we didn't die together, I'd die first. And I knew I could leap the fence from that world to this, a deer over barbed wire, to be with her. But this world to that. . . .

I lay on the grass against the frozen satin headstone. What I know about dying takes bookshelves to hold; what Leslie knew about it she could put in her evening bag with room left for her wallet and notebook. What a fool I had been to promise!

All right, Leslie, no suicide. But her death had left me less careful than ever I'd been. Late at night down narrow island spanways I drove her fluffy old Torrance sedan at speeds more suited to sports-cars, seat belt unfastened, remembering.

I spent money lavishly. A hundred thousand dollars for a Honda Starflash—seven hundred horsepower on a twelve-hundred-pound airframe, a hundred thousand dollars to fly wild in the weekend airenas, mock dogfights for local sports fans.

No suicide, I had said, but I never promised my wife that I wouldn't fly to win.

I dragged myself up from the grave, paced heavily to the house. Used to be, sunset was firecolors in the sky, Leslie a floating cloud of delight in what day's end did with her flowers, pointing me this, showing me that. Now it was gray everywhere.

Pye had told us we could find our way back into our own time. Why didn't she mention that the way home was a crash in the sea, and that one of us had to die?

Days I studied my death-books, bought more. So many people had crashed against this wall! Yet the only way it had ever been crossed was that side to this. If Leslie was with me, watching or listening, she gave no hint. No books toppled from our shelves, no pictures tilted on walls.

At night I pulled my pillow and sleeping bag out on the deck under the sky. I couldn't stand to sleep in our bed without her.

Sleep—once my schoolhouse, lecture hall, otherworld adventure-dome—now was lost shadows, clips from silent movies. Catch a glimpse of her, move to be with her, and I'd wake alone, desolate. Damn! *She should have studied!*

I flew those bizarre flights in the pattern over and over in my mind no matter how they hurt, a detective examining the body for clues. Somewhere there had to be an answer. Or else I'd die, promise or no.

The night was more brilliant than ever I'd seen, stars swirling into hours swirling into stars, as bright as that night with Le Clerc in old France. . . .

Know that ever about you stands the reality of love, and each moment you have the power to transform your world by what you have learned.

Fear not, nor be dismayed at the appearance that is darkness, at the empty cloak that is death.

Your own world is just as much a mirage as any other. Your oneness in love is reality, and mirages cannot change reality. Don't forget. No matter what seems to be. . . .

Wherever you go you're together, safe with the one you most love, at the point of all perspective.

You do not create your own reality. You create your own appearances.

You need her power. She needs your wings. Together, you fly!

Richie, it's easy. Just focus up!

I pounded my fist on the deck, furious, Attila's fiery spirit breaking loose to help me.

I don't care if we crashed, I thought, I don't even believe we crashed, we *didn't* goddamn crash! I don't care what I saw or heard or touched or tasted, I don't care for any evidence except life! Nobody is dead nobody is buried nobody is alone I have always been with her I am with her now I shall always be with her and she with me and nothing nothing nothing has the power to stand in our way!

I heard Leslie, a wisp of her cry: "Richie! *It's true!*"

There was no crash except in my mind, and I refuse to accept this lie for truth. I do not accept this so-called place I do not accept this so-called time there is no such thing as a goddamned Honda Starflash, Honda does not even make airplanes never has never will, I refuse to accept I'm not as good a psychic as she is, I know a thousand books to her none, goddammit, and I'll reach for that throttle and I'll shove the damn thing through the overhead if I have to, nobody crashed, nobody was thrown out, this is just another landing in the middle of that goddamned pattern and I have had enough of this belief of death and sorrow and crying on her grave and I *AM* going to show her I can do this, it is not impossible. . . .

I sobbed in fury, enormous power bursting through me, Samson pushing the pillars that held the world from falling. I felt it move, like bending iron, earthquakes splintered through the house. The stars shook, blurred. At once I drove my right arm forward.

The house vanished. Seawater thundered and poured away beneath our wings, Growly wrenched loose of the waves, broke free of the water and soared.

"Leslie! You're back! *We're together!*"

Her face was drenched in tears and laughter. "Richie, sweet darling!" she cried. "You did it, I love you, YOU DID IT!"

y husband left the other Richard sitting on the bed talking on the phone to his Leslie and slipped out to the balcony with me.

He kissed me and we held each other a long moment, so glad to be together, so glad to be us.

"Why don't you try the takeoff this time," I said. "You really, should know you can do it before we go home."

He reached for Growly's throttle, but nothing happened. Why should it be so hard for him, I wondered. Too many tracks in that mind, running at once.

"Richie, it's easy," I said. "Just focus up!"

I reached for the throttle myself, pushed it to show him how, and at once we started to move. It felt like it does when a scene in a film is finished and they're striking the set: what were mountains and forests turn into shaking cloth, rocks are bouncing sponges, heavy wheels roll onstage to trundle it all away.

"Let me try again," he said.

"OK, sweetie," I said. "I'll pull it back. Remember, the trick is *focus*. . . ."

It surprised me that we were so close to flying. The minute I brought the throttle back, Growly jumped into the air and there was water beneath us. The engine popped a few times, the way it would if it were too cold to fly. We zoomed up, then the nose dropped right back down again. He grabbed for the controls but it was too late.

It all seemed to be happening in slow motion. We crashed slowly; slowly came a storm of white noise, as though I dragged my finger over a phonograph needle with the volume full up; slowly there was water everywhere. Slowly the curtain came down and the lights dimmed to black.

When the world returned, it was murky green, no noise at all. Richard was clinging to the seaplane underwater, tearing pieces of it away, frantically trying to drag something loose while everything sank.

"Richie, no," I said. "We have a serious problem, we have to talk about it! There's nothing in the plane we care about anymore. . . ."

But sometimes he gets his mind set and first-things-first

doesn't matter to him, what matters is that he gets his old flying-jacket or whatever it is out of the airplane. He seemed terribly upset.

"All right, sweetie," I said. "Take your time. I'll wait for you."

I watched him fuss for a while, find what he was looking for. What an odd feeling! What he dragged out of the airplane was not his jacket, it was me, limp, hair streaming, like a drowned rat.

I watched him swim upward with my body, push my head above the water. "It's OK, sweet," he panted. "We're going to make it. . . ."

The fishing boat was nearly on top of him, sliding sideways the last few yards the same moment that a fellow jumped overboard, a rope tied to his waist. There was such panic on my dear Richard's face I couldn't look.

When I turned away I saw a glorious light, *love* expanding in front of me. It wasn't the tunnel Richard had told me so much about, but it felt that way because, compared to the light, everything else was ink and there was no direction but toward that astounding love.

The light said *don't worry*, such wondrous gentle perfect all-rightness I trusted it with my whole being.

Two figures were moving toward me. One was a teenaged boy, so familiar. . . . He stopped at a distance, stopped and stood motionless, watching.

The other figure moved closer, an older man no taller than I am. I knew that walk.

"Hello, Leslie," he said at last. The voice was deep and rough, charred from years of smoking.

"*Hy?* Hy Feldman, is that you?" I ran the last few steps to him and we threw our arms around each other and hugged and hugged, turning in circles, happy tears together.

No dearer friend did I have in all the world than this man who had stood with me in the old days when so many others had turned their backs. Couldn't start the day without a call to Hy.

We pulled away, looking at each other, smiles so big they hardly fit our faces. "Dear Hy! Oh, God, this is wonderful! I can't believe it! I'm so happy to see you again!"

When he had died three years ago . . . the shock and pain of that loss! And I had been so angry. . . .

At once I stood back, glared at him. "Hy, I'm furious with you!"

He smiled, eyes twinkling the way they used to. I had adopted him to be my wise older brother, he had chosen me for his headstrong sister.

"Still mad?"

"Of course I'm still mad! What a lousy, deceitful thing to do! I loved you! I trusted you! You *promised* not to smoke another cigarette as long as you lived, and then you went ahead and did and you broke *two* hearts with your cigarettes, Hy Feldman, you broke mine too! Did you ever stop to think about that? How much pain you gave all of us who loved you by doing something that took you from us so soon? And for such a stupid reason!"

He looked down sheepishly, glancing at me through those bushy eyebrows. "Do the words *I'm sorry* make a difference?"

"No," I pouted at him. "Hy, you could have died for a good reason, a good cause, and I would have understood, you know that. You could have died fighting for human rights, or to save the oceans or the forests — or to save some stranger's life. But you died to smoke cigarettes after you promised to quit!"

"Never again." He grinned at me. "I promise. . . ."

"Some promise," I said. I couldn't help but laugh.

"Does it seem like a long time?" he said.

"Yesterday," I said.

He took my hand, squeezed it and we turned toward the light. "Let's go. There's someone here you've been missing longer than you've missed me. . . ."

I stopped. Suddenly I could think of nothing but Richard. "Hy," I said, "I can't, I have to go back. Richard and I are in the middle of the most extraordinary adventure, we're seeing things, learning things . . . I can't wait to tell you! But something awful just happened! When I left him he was so upset he was frantic!" Now I was frantic, too. "I have to get back!"

"Leslie," he said, holding my hand tight, "Leslie, stop. I have something to tell you."

"*No!* Hy, please *no*. You're going to tell me I'm dead. Isn't that right?"

He nodded, that sad smile of his.

"But, Hy, I can't leave him, just disappear and never come back! We don't know how to live without each other."

He looked at me, gentle understanding, his smile gone.

"We talked about dying, what it's probably like," I told him, "and we never were afraid of death, it was being apart we were afraid of. We planned that somehow we'd die together, and we would have except for this stupid. . . . Can you imagine? I don't even know why we crashed!"

"It wasn't stupid," he said. "There was a reason."

"Well I don't know what the reason was and if I did it wouldn't matter. I can't leave him!"

"Have you thought that maybe he's got something to learn that he could never find if you were with him? Something important?"

I shook my head. "Nothing's that important," I said. "If it were, we'd have been apart before."

"You're apart now," he said.

"No! I do not accept that!"

At that moment I saw the young man moving toward us, hands in his pockets, head down. He was tall and thin and so shy I could see it in his walk. I could not look away, yet seeing him made such an ache in my heart that I could hardly stand.

Then he raised his head, mischievous black eyes smiling into mine again after all those years.

Ronnie!

My brother and I had been inseparable as children and now we clung to each other crying our desperate joy at being together again.

I'd been twenty, he'd been seventeen when he was killed in an accident, and I had mourned the loss until I was forty years old. He'd been so intensely *alive*, so impossible to imagine dead, I never could believe he was gone, couldn't accept it. Losing him had changed me from hopeful and determined to lost and wanting to die. What a powerful bond there had been between us!

Now we were together again and our happiness was as overwhelming as the pain had been.

"You're just the same," I told him finally, looking at him in amazement, remembering why I had never been able to watch a James Dean movie without crying, Ronnie's face so much like his. "How can you look the same after all this time?"

"That was so you'd know me." He laughed, thinking about other ideas he'd had for our reunion. "I thought about coming as an old dog or something, but . . . well, even *I* could see this wasn't the time for a joke."

Jokes. I'd been the deadly serious one, striving, driving, unstoppable. He'd decided our poverty was insurmountable, that there was no use struggling, and had chosen comic relief, laughing and playing pranks while I was at my most serious till sometimes I wanted to strangle him. Yet he was so charming, funny, handsome, he could get away with anything. Everyone loved him, especially me.

"How's Mom?" he asked. I felt that he knew, but wanted to hear it from me.

"Mom's fine," I said, "except she still misses you. I finally accepted that you were gone — about ten years ago, would you believe that? But she never could. Never."

He sighed.

Having refused to believe he was dead, now I could hardly believe he was there beside me. What an amazing thing, to be with him again! "There's so much to tell you, so much to ask. . . ."

"I told you something wonderful was waiting for you," Hy said. He put an arm around my shoulder and so did Ronnie, I hugged them both around the waist, and the three of us walked deeper into the light, arms around each other.

"Ronnie! Hy!" I shook my head, overcome again. "This is one of the happiest days of my life!"

Then I glimpsed what was ahead. "Oh . . . !"

A glorious valley spread into view as we walked, a narrow river sparkling between fields and forests filled with the golds and scarlets of autumn. Behind it, towering mountains were topped with snow. Waterfalls a thousand feet high fell silently in the distance. It was breathtaking, like the first time I had seen. . . .

"Yosemite?" I asked.

"We knew you loved it," Hy nodded, "so we thought you might like to sit here and talk."

We found a sunlit grove and sat on a carpet of leaves. We

stared at each other, pure joy. Where to begin, I thought, where to begin?

Another part of me knew, asked the question that had haunted me for years.

"Ronnie, why? I know it was an accident, I know you didn't die on purpose. But I've been learning how much we control our lives, and I can't help thinking that on some level you chose to leave when you did."

The answer came as if he'd thought about it as long as I had. "It was a poor choice," he said, easily. "I thought I had such a bad start in that life that I could never make it better. For all my jokes, I was a lost soul, did you know that?" He smiled his devilish smile to cover the sadness.

"I guess deep down, I did," I said, my heart breaking all over again, "and that's what I never could accept. How could you be lost when we all loved you so much?"

"I didn't like me as much as you did," he said, "didn't feel I deserved loving or anything else, for that matter. Looking back now I know it could have been a good life, but I couldn't see that then." He looked away. "It wasn't that I went out and said I'm going to kill myself, you know, but I didn't try very hard to live, either. I didn't bash away at life like you did." He shook his head. "Poor choice."

He was more serious than I had ever seen him. How strange and comforting it was to hear him talk like this, my confusion and the pain of decades gone with a few words of explanation.

He smiled at me shyly. "I kept an eye on you," he said. "For a while I thought you were going to join me right away. Then I saw you turn it around, saw I could have done it too and wished . . . well, it was a tough lifetime. I should have handled it differently. I learned a lot, though. Used it ever since."

"You kept an eye on me?" I said. "You know what's been going on in my life? You know about Richard?" I was thrilled to think that he knew about my husband.

He nodded. "It's just great. I'm happy for you!"

Richard!

Suddenly the panic was back. How could I sit here *talking* like this? What was *wrong* with me? Richard had told me people went through a time of confusion just after death, but this was unthinkable! "He's worried about me, you know. He thinks he's lost me, that we've lost each other. I can't stay, much as I love you both, I can't! You understand, don't you? I have to go back to him. . . ."

"Leslie," Hy said, "Richard won't be able to see you."

"Why not?" What terrible thing did he know that I hadn't considered? Was I now the ghost of a ghost? Was I. . . . "Are you saying . . . do you mean to say I'm really dead? That this isn't near-death, where I have the choice to go back, but *dead*? No choice?"

He nodded.

I stopped, stunned. "But Ronnie's been with me, he said he kept an eye on me, he's been there all along. . . ."

"You couldn't see him, though, could you?" asked Hy. "You didn't know he was there."

"Sometimes in dreams. . . ."

"Of course in dreams," he said, "but. . . ."

I felt sudden relief. "Good!"

"Is that the kind of marriage you want?" he said. "Richard will see you when he's asleep, he'll forget you every morning? Instead of getting ready to meet him when he comes here, teach him what you've learned, you want to float around him unseen?"

"Hy, for all the talk we had about dying and going on past death, about our mission together over lifetimes, as far as he knows I was killed in a plane crash and that was the end of me! He'll think everything he believes is wrong!"

My old friend watched me, incredulous. Why couldn't he understand? "Hy, the reason we lived was to be together, to express love. We weren't finished! It's like writing a book and quitting midword halfway through chapter seventeen of a twenty-four-chapter book. We don't just quit and make believe that's the end! Let that book be published, some useless thing with no ending?" I refused to accept it.

"And a reader comes along who wants to find out what we learned, wants to see how creatively we used what we knew to conquer the challenges we were given, and in the middle of the book it stops and there's an editor's note: *Then they crashed their seaplane and she was killed so they never finished what they started.*"

"Most people's lives aren't finished. Mine wasn't," said Hy.

"You're right about that!" I flared at him. "So you know how it feels. We're not going to end our story in the middle!"

He smiled at me, that warm smile. "You want your story to say that after the crash Leslie came back from the dead and they lived happily ever after?"

"It wouldn't be the worst line a book ever had." We all laughed. "Of course I'd hope it might say how we did it, what principles we used, so anyone else could do the same thing."

I'd meant it as a joke, but suddenly it occurred to me that this might be one more test, one more challenge in the pattern.

"Look, Hy," I said, "Richard's been right about so many of these things that seem crazy at first. You know his cosmic law about holding things in thought and having them come true. Is cosmic law suddenly changed because we crashed? How can it be possible for me to hold something in my thought now, something this important, and *not* have it come true?"

I could see him give in. He smiled. "Cosmic laws don't change."

I reached out and squeezed his hand. "For a little while, I thought you were going to try to stop me."

"Nobody on earth had the power to stop Leslie Parrish. What makes you think they can do it here?"

We stood and Hy hugged me goodbye. "I'm curious," he said. "If Richard had died and not you, would you have let him go, would you have trusted he'd be all right for however long it took you to finish your own lifetime?"

"No. I'd shoot myself."

"Head like a rock," he said.

"I know it doesn't make sense. Nothing makes sense but I have to get back to him. I can't leave him, Hy. I love him!"

"I know. Off you go. . . ."

I turned to Ronnie. My precious brother and I held each other a long quiet time. How hard it was to pull away!

"I love you," I said, biting my lip against tears, backing away. "I love both of you. I'll always love you. And we'll be together again, won't we?"

"You know it," said Ronnie. "You'll die and look for your brother again, and here comes this old dog. . . ."

I laughed through tears.

"We love you too," he said.

I had never really believed this day could happen. Under my skeptic's hat I had hoped Richard was right, that there was more to living than one lifetime. Now I knew. Now, with what I had learned from the pattern and from dying, I walked away certain of it. I knew, too, that someday Richard and I would walk into this light together. Not now.

Returning to life wasn't impossible, wasn't even hard. Once through the wall that assumes we never dare the impossible, I saw the pattern in the tapestry, the way Pye had said. Thread by thread, step by step! I wasn't returning to life, I was returning to a focus of form, and that's a focus we change every day.

I found my dear Richard in an alternate world he had somehow taken for real. He was crumpled on the ground over my grave. His grief was a solid wall around him, he could neither see nor hear that I was with him.

I pushed against the wall. "Richard. . . ."

Nothing.

"Richard, *I'm here!*"

He sobbed on my headstone. Hadn't we agreed, *no stones*?

"Dear one, I am with you this minute as you cry on the ground, I will be with you when you sleep and when you wake. We're separated only by your belief that we're apart!"

Wildflowers on the grave told him life covers the very spot where death can only seem, but he no more heard their message than mine.

He dragged himself up at last, sorrowed toward the house, his wall of grief around him. He missed the sunset shouting to him that what seems night is the world getting ready for a dawn that already exists. He threw his sleeping bag on the deck.

How much shouting can one man block from knowing? Was this my husband, my dear Richard convinced that nothing happens by chance, from the fall of a leaf to the birth of a galaxy? Crying his heart out on his sleeping bag, under the stars?

"Richard!" I said. "You're right! You've been right all along! The crash was not by chance! Perspective! You already know everything you need to bring us together again! Remember? *Focus!*"

243

All at once, he pounded his fist on the deck, raging against his walls.

"We're not finished," I cried to him. "Our story isn't over! We have . . . so much . . . to live for. *You can change now! Dear Richard, NOW!*"

The wall around him shifted, cracked at the edges. I closed my eyes, focused with all my being. I saw the two of us in Growly's undamaged cockpit, afloat above the pattern, I felt us together again. No grief, no sorrow, no separation.

He felt it, too. He strained to press the throttle forward. His eyes were closed, and every fiber of his body trembled against that simple lever.

As though he had been hypnotized, breaking out of his trance now by sheer will, he shuddered, muscled every ounce against his own iron beliefs. The beliefs bent one quarter of an inch. Half an inch.

My heart nearly burst for him. I added my will to his. "Dear one! I'm not dead and I never was! I am with you this minute! We're together!"

The walls shattered around him, pieces falling away. Growly's motor perked, purred. Instrument pointers moved ever so slightly.

He held his breath, the veins pulsed on his neck, his jaw locked tight, wrestling to shift what he had taken for truth. He refused the crash. Against all the evidence of appearances, he refused my death.

"Richie!" I cried to him. "*It's true! Please yes! We still can fly!*"

And then the throttle gave way, the engine wound up into thunder, spray flew beneath us.

It was glory to see him! His eyes opened in the second that Growly burst from the waves.

I heard his voice at last in a world we shared again.

"Leslie! You're back! *We're together!*"

"Richie, sweet darling!" I cried. "You did it, I love you, YOU DID IT!"

good way to fall on your nose, flying airplanes, is to pull the control wheel back after takeoff and hold it there. But we were swept with the joy of resurrection — Growly's wings could have fallen off and we would have climbed like rockets.

I held her, felt her arms around me as we climbed.

"Leslie!" I cried. "I'm not dreaming! *You're not dead!*"

She wasn't killed, she wasn't buried on the hillside, she was with me, radiant as sunrise. The dream was not this moment, it had been those months believing that she had died, months mourning alone in that alternate time.

"Without you it was. . . ." I said. "The world stopped. Nothing mattered!" I touched her face. "Where *were* you?"

She laughed through tears. "I was with you!" she said. "When we sank, I watched you underwater. I saw you pull my body out of the airplane. I thought you were after your jacket and I couldn't *believe* when I saw what it was! I was right there with you, but you wouldn't see me, all you could see was my body!"

She *had* been with me.

After everything we'd learned together, what made me suddenly forget and take appearances for real? My first word at her death was *NO!* One word, instant truth. Why didn't I listen? How different it would have been if I had refused to believe the lie at once instead of later!

"I could have helped you," I said, "if I'd held to what I knew was true. . . ."

She shook her head. "It would have been a miracle not to focus on what you saw in the crash. And later the grief was like a wall around you. I couldn't get through. If I'd been quicker, maybe I could have. . . ."

"Damn me! A test like that, and I failed!"

"You didn't fail!" She hugged me again. "You were wonderful! In spite of everything you saw through it, you pushed Growly's throttle, you brought us out of that world by yourself, do you realize that? You did it!"

So swiftly in that terrible world-of-her-death had I begun to forget the sound of her voice, the sight of her. Finding her now was the delight of meeting love all over again.

"There's so much to tell you!" she said. "I know it's only been an hour or so, but so much. . . ."

"An *hour*? Wookie, it's been *months!* Three months and a week!"

"No, Richie, an hour and a half at most!" She looked puzzlement at me. "I left right in the middle of. . . ." She caught her breath, her eyes sparkled. "Oh, Richard, I saw Ronnie! It was like he never died, he was just the same. And dear Hy, too! Hy met me first, he told me it was all right, you and I would be together soon, no matter what. And right after the crash, there was this beautiful light, just like in your death-books. . . ."

It used to be, I'd drive to town for groceries, come home and it would take us an hour to catch up on all that had happened while we were apart. This latest journey, an hour in her perception, three months in mine—how long would it take to tell?

"It's the most glorious place, Richie!" she said. "If it weren't for you, I would never have come back!" She thought for a moment. "Tell me. Would it have made a difference to you if you'd known I was all right, that I was happy, that I was with people I loved?"

"If I knew you were safe and happy, yes," I said. "I think so. I could have thought of it as a . . . a transfer, as if you had gone ahead of me, moved to our new town, our new home, to learn the rules and streets and people while I finished our work here, it would have helped some. But it *isn't* a transfer. There's no mail, there's no phone, there's no way to *know*!"

"Without the grief," she said, "I think we might have talked.

We could have met in meditations, in dreams, but you were bottled up in sorrow. . . ."

"If it ever happens again, I'll remember. I'll know you're there, no matter what. And you remember, too!"

She nodded. "There's so much to learn from this—so many puzzles to solve!" she said. "It's been thirty years since Ronnie died. How could he be there waiting for me? With so many lifetimes, why wasn't he off in some other . . . incarnations?"

"But he is, and so are we," I said. "Look down there." The pattern turned below us. There was no end to it, and there never would be. "All those lives at once, and after-lives and between-lives, too. Don't you believe it yet? Don't you think it's true?"

"I'm not sure what I believe now," she smiled, "but I know I saw my brother again. He was always full of jokes, and he was silly as ever. He said. . . ." She burst out laughing. "He said next time we meet . . . he's going to show up . . . as an old. . . ." She laughed till she lost her breath.

"An old what?"

". . . an old dog!"

I didn't understand, but whatever Ronnie had said, it had been enough to turn his sister helpless, remembering, and I laughed with her. What a strange pleasure it was to laugh again!

In the pattern below there must be an alternate us, I thought, who failed to make the leap to find each other. I didn't speak the thought to Leslie to keep from breaking our hearts all over again.

We talked through what had happened, tried to piece it together. Not all of it made sense, but some did.

"It seemed so real!" I said. "I wasn't a ghost, I wasn't walking through walls, people saw me, knew me, our house was just the same." I thought about the place. "Not quite," I said, noticing now what I'd failed to notice in those months apart. "It was our house, but it was different somehow, and I never questioned the difference. And the car—it wasn't our old Chrysler, it was a *Torrance*. Isn't that odd?"

"Without the practice we've had in the pattern, I think you'd still be living there," she said. "If we'd grown up in that alternate place without just having jumped in and out of ten lifetimes, if we were convinced that the world with 1976 Torrances is the only one that exists. . . . If I died in that world, could you have broken out? Even to bring us together again? Could you ever have overcome the belief of dying?"

"What a question!" I said. "I don't know."

"Richie, we barely made it as it was! After everything we learned, we barely made it!"

She watched the maze below us. "Are we trapped here? Is it as hard to get out of this place as it was to *overcome death*?"

Now safe together again, past the worst test of our lives, we looked at each other, a single thought in mind: before anything else happens, we have to find our way home.

"Remember what Pye said?" I asked. "The pattern is psychic,

but the way back is spiritual? She said guide yourself by hope."

I frowned, though, thinking about it. How do we guide ourselves by hope? We hoped to go home, why weren't we there?

"She didn't say hope, wookie," Leslie said at last. "She said love! She said guide yourself by love!"

19

Sure enough, Pye was right: it's
easy to be led by love.

Those two on their way to the meeting in Los Angeles—
their little planet might be a mirage, but it was *their* mirage,
the canvas they had chosen to paint the sunrise as they saw
it, and they loved what they were painting. We concentrated
on that love.

"Ready?" asked Leslie.

I took her hand, and together we touched the control wheels
in front of us. Eyes closed, we focused our hearts on those
two in their world, on their way to their own new discov-
eries. As we loved each other, so we loved our home, flew to

give it what we'd seen and learned. It wasn't my hand that moved the controls, or Leslie's; it was the controls that moved our hands, as though Growly had become a living thing, knowing the way to fly.

After a while our flying-boat slowed, banked into a wide turn. I opened my eyes to see Leslie opening hers.

We saw it at once. Below us, underwater, amidst all the twists and fans of the pattern, lay a golden figure eight. It was the same curving path that Pye had drawn in the sand between Threat City and the town of Peace.

"Pye said we can give hints to other aspects of ourselves. . . ." I said.

". . . and there's our hint!" said Leslie. "Dear Pye!"

The moment we turned our minds from love, we were on our own again, as if a spell had been broken. Growly changed from partner into servant, asking for guidance. I touched the wheel to the right to continue our circle above the golden sign, pulled the power back, made the final turn toward the place. Wind ruffled the surface and the gold danced.

"Wheels are up, flaps are down."

It was a simple task, landing the seaplane on the mark. We flew into the wind a few inches above the water, hanging on the Seabird's stalling speed. Just before we reached the spot, I cut the power and Growly splashed down.

At once the pattern vanished and there we were neat as pins in the other Growly, aloft over Los Angeles.

But we weren't the pilots, we were back-seat passengers again, ghosts along for the ride! Ahead of us sat the two that we had been, watching the sky for other airplanes, setting the transponder code for the descent to Santa Monica. Beside me, Leslie would have cried out, clapped her hand over her mouth instead.

"Four six four five?" said Richard the pilot.

"There," said his wife. "What would you do without me?"

They hadn't seen us.

The instant I slammed our ghostly throttle forward I felt Leslie's hand on mine, the same fright in her. In agonizing slow motion, as we sat unbreathing, the scene blurred and disappeared.

Once more we were tearing along through the wavelets above the pattern, and a touch on the wheel launched us into the air.

We looked astonished at each other, breathed at the same time.

"Richie, no! I was sure that would be the one place we could land without being ghosts!"

I looked down as we turned, found the golden symbol. "It's right there, and we can't get home!"

I glanced behind us, hoping for Pye. It wasn't insight we needed now, just simple instructions. She wasn't there with either. The sign under the waves was a combination lock into our own time, but we didn't know the numbers.

"There's no way out!" said Leslie. "Everywhere we land, we're ghosts!"

"Except for Lake Healey. . . ."

"Pye was at Lake Healey," she said. "That doesn't count."

". . . and the crash."

"The crash?" she said. "*I* was a ghost! Even *you* couldn't see me." She fell into thought, trying to put it together.

I switched to a left circle around the gold to keep it in sight on my side of the airplane. It seemed to waver underwater, fading as though it were a symbol in mind instead of in the pattern, melting as our focus on love gave way to anxiety. I leaned toward it, intent.

It was fading, all right. Pye, help! I thought. Without the marker, it wouldn't matter whether we knew the combination or not. I began memorizing the many-branching crossroad beneath it. We couldn't lose this place!

". . . but I wasn't an observer-ghost," Leslie went on, "I believed I had died because of the crash. I believed I was a *real* ghost and so I was. Richie, you're right, the crash is the answer!"

"We're all ghosts here, wookie," I said, still memorizing. "It's all appearances, every bit of it. . . ." Two branches to the left, six to the right, two nearly straight ahead. The sign was gradually rippling away and I didn't want to tell her.

"The world we crashed into was real to you," she said. "You believed you survived, so you weren't a ghost! It was a paral-

255

lel time but you buried my body, you lived in a house, you flew airplanes and drove cars and talked to people. . . ."

All at once I realized what she was saying. I looked at her, stunned. "To get back home, you want to *crash the airplane again?* Pye told us it would be *easy,* it would be like falling off a log! She didn't say anything about *crashing Growly.* . . ."

"No, she didn't. But there was something about the crash . . . why weren't you a ghost afterward? What was different about that one landing?"

"*Overboard!*" I said. "We weren't detached observers on the surface, we were part of the pattern, we were in it!"

I turned back to find the last glow of the gold dissolving; circled the spot I had memorized. "Worth a try?"

"Try what? You mean . . . while we're still flying, you want to *jump overboard?*"

I kept my eyes on the spot where the symbol had been. "Yes! We start to land, we let the airplane slow down, then just as we touch the water, we step out the door!"

"My God, Richard, that's terrifying!"

"The pattern is a world of metaphor, and the metaphor works, don't you see? To become a part of any time, to take it seriously, we have to submerge ourselves in it. Remember what Pye said about floating above the pattern, uninvolved? And falling off a log? She was telling us how to get home! *Growly's the log!*"

"I can't do it!" she said. "*I can't!*"

"Slow flight, against the wind," I said, "we'll be down to thirty miles per hour. I'd rather step over the side than crash. . . ." I turned to final approach, made ready to land.

She followed my gaze. "What are you watching?"

"The marker's gone. I don't want to lose sight of the place where it was."

"*Gone?*" She looked across me at the empty place below.

"OK," she said. "If you jump, I'll jump. But once we let go, there's no getting back!"

I swallowed, never taking my eyes from the place we had to touch down. "We'll have to unfasten our seat belts, open the canopy, climb out and let go. Can you do that?"

"Maybe we could unfasten the belts and unlock the canopy now," she said.

We released our seat belts and a second later I heard the roar of wind as she unlocked the canopy. My throat went dry again.

She leaned toward me, kissed my cheek. "Wheels are up, flaps are down," she said. "I'm ready when you are."

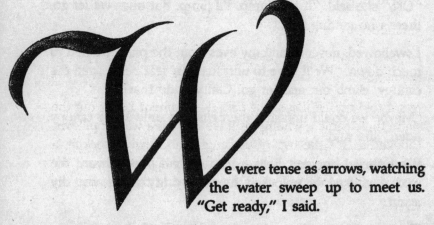

e were tense as arrows, watching the water sweep up to meet us. "Get ready," I said.

"When we touch, it's open the door and jump," she said, rehearsing it one more time.

"Right!"

"Don't forget!" she said, holding the canopy handle tight.

"Don't you forget either," I said, "no matter what seems to be!"

The keel of the flying-boat clipped the waves. I closed my eyes, not to be fooled by appearances.

CANOPY.

I could feel Leslie push up at the same time as I did, the wind roaring against us.

JUMP!

I hurled myself overboard, and in that instant opened my eyes. We had leaped from our airplane not into water but into empty air, we were tumbling together, no parachutes, straight down over Los Angeles.

"LESLIE!"

Her eyes were closed, she didn't hear me over the howl of the wind.

Lies, I told myself, *I'm seeing lies.* The moment I shut out the sight, there came a whomp as if we had hit a wall of pillows. I looked to see the two of us caught in Growly's cockpit, a silent shell of golden light exploding away, and gone. We were in the pilots' seats this time, purring through the sky safe as cats on a carpet.

"*Richie, we made it!*" she cried, throwing her arms around me with a shriek of delight. "We made it! You're a genius!"

"Anything we believed in would have worked," I said modestly, although I wasn't sure of that. If she insists it's genius, I thought, I'll have to agree.

"It doesn't matter," she said joyfully. "We're back!"

We were heading 142 degrees, magnetic compass steady southeast, nav instruments humming, loran glowing orange numbers. The back seat was empty. The only pattern beneath us now was streets and rooftops, the only water below glittered blue from backyard swimming pools.

She pointed to two airplanes in the distance. "Traffic there," she said, "and there."

"Got 'em," I said.

We looked at the radios at the same time. "Shall we try . . . ?"

She nodded, fingers crossed.

"Hi, Los Angeles Approach," I said, "Seabird One Four Bravo. Do you have us painted on your radar?"

"Affirmative. One Four Bravo is radar contact, you have traffic at one o'clock, two miles, northbound, altitude unknown."

The controller didn't ask where we had been, didn't hint we had disappeared from his screen for a quarter of a year, didn't hear the chorus of cheers and hurrays in Growly's cockpit.

Leslie touched my knee. "Tell me what you saw when we first. . . ."

"A sky as blue as flowers, a shallow-water ocean over the pattern. Pye, Jean-Paul, Ivan and Tatiana, Linda and Krys. . . ."

"OK," she said, shaking her head. "Not a dream. It happened."

We flew on to Santa Monica like Scrooges returned, delighted for the Christmas of this lifetime.

"What if it's true?" said Leslie. "What if everybody everywhere is some aspect of who we are, and we're some aspect of them? How will that change the way we live?"

"Good question," I said. The ten-mile mark lit up on the loran. I eased the nose down a little more, trimmed to hold it there. "Good question. . . ."

We landed on the broad single runway at Santa Monica Airport, taxied the amphibian to a parking spot, shut down the engine. I halfway expected the scene to jump a thousand years when we rolled to a stop, but not so. It remained: scores of other airplanes parked quietly about us, the hush of traffic on Centinela Boulevard, salt air and sunlight.

I helped my wife from the plane. We stood for a long moment on the surface of our own planet, in our own time, and we held each other.

"Are you awed?" I whispered into her hair.

She pulled back to look into my eyes, nodded.

I lifted our bags out of the airplane, we stretched the canopy cover over the windshield, fastened it tight.

Across the parking ramp the line-boy left a half-polished Luscombe Silvaire, climbed into a fuel truck and rumbled to a halt in front of the Seabird.

He was a kid, no older than I had been when I had the job, wore the same kind of leather jacket I had fancied then, though his had the word DAVE stitched above the left breast pocket. How easy to see myself in him, I thought, how much we could tell him of his futures already true, of the adventures this moment waiting his choice!

"Afternoon, folks," he said. "Welcome to Santa Monica! Would you like a little fuel today?"

We laughed. How strange to need fuel again!

"Sure would," I said. "It's been a long flight."

"Where-all have you been?" he asked.

I looked at my wife for help, but she didn't volunteer, listened casually for my answer. "Oh, just flying around," I said lamely.

Dave wrestled a lever, engaged the truck's fuel pump. "I haven't flown a Seabird yet," he said, "but I hear they can land nearly anywhere. Is that true?"

"It's true, all right," I said. "This airplane will take you anywhere you can imagine."

21

*I*t wasn't till we were safely in our rental car, on the way to the hotel, that either of us raised the question.

"Well," said Leslie as she hummed us up the on-ramp to the Santa Monica Freeway. "Do we talk about this or not?"

"At the conference?"

"Anywhere," she said.

"What do we say? A funny thing happened on the way to the meeting: we got stopped midair for three months locked in a dimension where there isn't any space or time except sometimes it seems like there is and we found that everybody is an aspect of everybody else because consciousness is one and by the way the future of the world is subjective and we pick what's going to happen to the whole world by what we choose to bring true for ourselves thank you very much and are there any questions?'"

She laughed. "As soon as a few people in this country agree it may not be impossible for a person to have more than one lifetime, here we come saying no, everybody has an *infinite* number of lifetimes and they're all going on at once! Better not get into that. Let's keep what happened to ourselves."

"It's not new," I said. "Remember what Albert Einstein said? *For us believing physicists*, he said, *the distinction between past, present and future is only an illusion, even if a stubborn one.*"

"*Albert Einstein* said that?"

"That's not the half of it! Whenever you want something incredible, ask your physicist. Light bends; space warps; clocks on rockets run slower than clocks at home; split one particle and get two the same size; fire your rifle at the speed of light and nothing comes out of the barrel. . . . It's not like we're springing this on the world, you and me. Anyone who reads quantum mechanics, anyone who's ever played with Schroedinger's cat. . . ."

"But how many Schroedinger's-cat lovers do you know?" she said. "How many people curl up on a cold night with their calculus and their quantum physics? I don't think we should talk about it. I don't think anyone would believe us. It happened to us and even *I* wonder if it's true."

"Dear skeptic," I said. But I wondered, too. What if it were all a dream, a rare mutual dream, the pattern and Pye and . . . what if it were all fantasy?

I squinted my eyes at the traffic, testing our new perspective. Was it us in the black-glass Mercedes limousine? Us in the rusted Chevrolet stopped at the roadside, radiator steaming? Us there just-married? Us alongside frowning, on the way to the scene of some crime-to-be, murder in our hearts? We tried to see them as us in other bodies, couldn't make it work. Each was separate and unknown, cocooned in rolling steel. I could as little imagine us in luxury as I could in poverty, though we'd lived through both. We're just us, I thought, and nobody else.

"Are you *starved*?" said Leslie.

"I haven't eaten in months."

"Can you last to Robertson Boulevard?"

"I can if you can," I said.

Leslie sped along the freeway, then eased toward the exit onto streets left over from her life in Hollywood. That lifetime was further gone than Le Clerc's, for all the connection she said she felt to it.

Sometimes when we curled in bed late nights watching old films, she'd hug me without warning and say, "Thank you for taking me away from all that!" Yet I suspected a part of her missed it, though she never admitted that unless the film was very good.

The restaurant was still there: a vegetarian smoke-free classical-music paradise for the conscientious hungry. It had become popular in the years since we had left the city, and the nearest parking spot was a block away.

She got out of the car and set off briskly toward the restaurant. "I used to live here! Can you believe it? How many lifetimes ago?"

"You can't say *ago*," I said, taking her hand to slow her. "Though I have to admit it's easier to understand serial lifetimes than simultaneous ones. First old Egypt, then a romp through the Han dynasty, open the Wild West. . . ."

On the way to the restaurant we passed a grand new media center, its window a wall of television sets all running at once, confusion stacked four deep.

". . . but what we've just learned, that's not so easy."

Leslie glanced in the window, then stopped so suddenly I thought she had forgotten her purse, or broken the heel of her shoe. One moment starving, racing for the restaurant, the next she was at a full halt, watching television.

"All our lifetimes at once?" she said, lost in those screens. "Jean-Paul Le Clerc lifetimes and end-of-the-world lifetimes and different-universe Mashara lifetimes all going on at once and we don't know how to say it, or even how to grasp it?"

"Mm. Not easy," I admitted. "How about something to eat?"

She tapped the glass of the window. "Look."

Every set inside was tuned to a different channel, and at that moment of the afternoon they were tuned mostly to old movies.

In one screen Scarlett O'Hara swore never to be hungry again; in the next Cleopatra schemed for Mark Antony; beneath her danced Fred and Ginger, a whirl of top hat and chiffon; to their right flew Bruce Lee, a streak of dragon vengeance; nearby Captain Kirk and lovely Lieutenant Paloma outwitted a space god; to their left a dashing knight threw magic crystals that turned his kitchen sparkling clean.

Other dramas in other screens lined the window along the sidewalk. From each screen dangled a crimson sale tag: BUY ME!

"Simultaneous!" I said.

"So past or future doesn't depend on what year it is," she said, "it depends on which channel's tuned in . . . *it depends on what we choose to watch!*"

"An infinite number of channels," I said, interpreting the window, "but no set can play more than one channel at a time, so each one's convinced it's the only channel there is!"

She pointed past me. "New set."

In the other corner of the window, a high-tech console showed Spencer Tracy puzzled by Katharine Hepburn, while a five-inch insert in the picture raced a heap of stock cars toward the finish line.

"Aha!" I said. "If we're advanced enough, we can tune in more than one lifetime!"

"How do we get so advanced?" she wondered.

"We cost more?"

She laughed. "I knew there was a way."

267

We walked on, arms around each other, turned in at our old haunt, found a booth.

She opened the menu, hugged it. "Roots-of-heaven salad!" she said.

"Some things never change," I said.

She nodded happily.

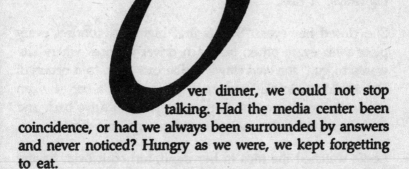

ver dinner, we could not stop talking. Had the media center been coincidence, or had we always been surrounded by answers and never noticed? Hungry as we were, we kept forgetting to eat.

"It's not coincidence," I said. "Everything's a metaphor when we think about it."

"Everything?"

"Try me," I said. "After what we've learned, anything you can name . . . I can show you what it's trying to teach us." Even to me it sounded brash.

She glanced at a seascape painted across the room. "The ocean," she said.

"The ocean has many drops of water," I told her, barely needing to think, the idea as clear in mind as though it were a crystal from Atkin floating before me. "Boiling drops and icy ones, bright ones and dark, drops that fly in the air and drops squeezed in tons of pressure. Drops that change from one moment to the next, drops that vaporize and condense. Each drop is one with the ocean. Without the ocean, the drops cannot exist. Without drops, the ocean cannot be. But a drop in the ocean, you can't call it a 'drop.' There's no boundary between drops until somebody draws one!"

"Very good!" she said. "That's very good, Richie!"

I looked at my placemat, a map of Los Angeles. "Streets and highways," I said.

She closed her eyes. "Streets and highways connect every place with every other, but each driver chooses where she wants to go," she said slowly. "She can drive to a beautiful countryside or to skid row, to a university or a bar, she can follow the road over the horizon or she can drive back and forth in a rut or she can park and not go anywhere."

Leslie watched the idea in her mind, turned it over, having fun. "She can choose her climate by where she drives, Fairbanks or Mexico City or Rio, she can drive safely or recklessly, she can drive a race car or a sedan or a truck, she can keep it in perfect shape or let it go to pieces. She can drive without a map and make every turn a surprise or she can plan exactly where she's going and know just how she's going to get there. Every road she will take is already there, before she drives on it and after she's gone past. Every possible trip already exists, and the driver is one with them all.

She just chooses, every morning, which trip she'll take that day."

"WOW! Perfect!"

"Did we just learn this," she said, "or have we always known and never asked?" Before I could guess she tested me again. "Arithmetic."

We couldn't make it work with everything, but we could with nearly any system or interest or vocation. Computer programming, film-making, retail sales, bowling, manufacturing, flying, gardening, engineering, art, education, sailing . . . behind every calling lay a metaphor with the same serene view of the way the universe works.

"Leslie, do you have the feeling. . . . Are we the same people now that we were before?"

"I don't think so," she said. "If we came back unchanged after what happened we'd be . . . but that's not what you mean, is it?"

"I mean *really different*," I said, keeping my voice low. "Look at the people around us, the people in the restaurant."

She did, for the longest time. "Maybe it's going to fade, but. . . ."

". . . we know everyone here," I said.

At the table next to us sat a woman from Viet Nam, grateful for kind cruel hateful loving America, proud of her two daughters working like wonders at the tops of their school classes. We understood, we were proud with her, and of what she had done to make hope come true in their lives.

Across the room, four teenagers laughed and slapped at each other, ignoring all but themselves, begging attention for reasons they didn't know. Those awkward, painful years from our own lives echoed in our hearts, instant understanding.

There a young man crammed for finals, oblivious to everything but the page in front of him, following graphs with his pencil. He knew he'd probably not chart I-beam bending-moments ever again, but he knew as well that it's the path that's important, and every step along it matters. We knew, too.

A white-haired couple, neatly dressed, murmured at a corner booth. So much to remember from what we did with a life-time, so warm a feeling to have done the best we knew and to plan for futures no one else could imagine.

"What an odd feeling," I said.

"Yes," she said. "Has it ever happened before?"

A few out-of-body experiences, I thought, had a certain cosmic unity. But never had I felt at one with people while I was wide awake, sitting in a restaurant. "Not like this. I don't think so." Memories scattered from as far back as I could remember, a gossamer connection to everyone else underlying what seemed to be our differences.

One, Pye had said. Hard to criticize, I thought, hard to judge when it's ourselves in the spotlight. No need for judging when we already understand.

One. Instead of strangers, are these the kids we were, the knowing souls we've yet to be? A focus of intimate expectant curiosity spanned one of us to another, wordless calm delight at our power to build lifetimes and adventures and yearnings to know.

One. Across the city, were they us too? Undiscovered and superstar, drug dealer and cop, attorney and terrorist and studio musician?

That gentle understanding stayed with us as we talked. It's not the knowing that comes and goes, I thought, it's our awareness that it's there. What we see is our own consciousness, and when that's lifted up, how our scenes do change! Everyone in this world—we're reflections, we're living mirrors of each other.

"I think a lot more has happened to us than we begin to realize," said Leslie.

"It feels as if our trolley is rolling over a million switches," I said, "and we're watching the tracks change under us. Where do we come out, where are we headed?"

Dark came down outside while we talked. We felt like lovers meeting again in paradise—we were the same people we had always been, but now we had glimpsed who we had been before, seen what might happen in lives we had yet to know.

At last we left the restaurant. Arms around each other, we walked into the night and into the city. Autos hushed north-southeastwest in the streets; a boy on a skateboard swerved graceful highspeed around us, wheels roaring; a young couple moved toward us in silent rapture, holding each other close; all of us on our way to meet this minute's, this evening's, this lifetime's choices.

23

At eight forty-five the next morning, we followed a tree-lined drive to the top of the hill and entered a parking garden, space for automobiles among the flowers. We followed one of many paths to our meeting hall through drifts of daffodils and tulips and hyacinths, tiny silver flowers shining among them, delicate scents in the air. Spring Hill, indeed!

In the building, a spacious multi-windowed room lay before us, cantilevered over the sea. Sunlight danced on the water below, reflecting patterns to the ceiling.

Two rows of chairs spread in a broad arc across the room, a wide aisle between them. Past the chairs was a low platform, three lime-green blackboards, a microphone on a silver stand.

We stopped at a table in the entry. It held only two name-tags, two information packets, notebooks and pens: ours. We were the last to arrive, the last of fifty or so who had traveled thousands of miles to come to this meeting of minds.

Men and women stood among the chairs, saying hello; one stooped at the center blackboard, wrote a topic and her name.

A burly gentleman, black hair streaked with gray, walked to the platform. "Welcome," he said firmly into the microphone, over the talk in the room. "Welcome to Spring Hill. It looks like we're all here. . . ."

He waited while we found our chairs and sat down. Leslie and I finished smoothing on our nametags, looked up at the same moment to the speaker. The room blurred in shock.

I turned to her in the same instant she turned to me. "Richie! It's. . . ."

The speaker walked to the center blackboard, reached for chalk. "Has anyone not listed the title of their talk? The Bachs, just arrived, your talk . . . ?"

"*ATKIN!*" I said.

"Call me Harry," he said. "Do you have a title for your talk?"

It felt as though we were back in the pattern, landed in some annex to the idea-foundry. Except for the mark of a few years, the man was the same. Was this not the Los Angeles that we thought it was, had we somehow missed. . . .

"No," I said, shaken. "No title. No talk."

Heads turned for a moment. Faces of strangers, and yet. . . .

Leslie touched my hand. "It can't be," she whispered. "But what a coincidence!"

Of course. Harry Atkin had invited us, it was his signature on the letter that had brought us here, we knew his name before we had left home. But he looked so much like Atkin!

"Anyone else?" he asked. "Fifteen-minute maximum, remember, for the first round of talks. Six talks and a fifteen-minute break, six more and a one-hour lunch. Any other titles?"

A woman stood, a few chairs ahead of us.

Atkin nodded to her. "Marsha?"

"Is Artificial Intelligence Artificial? A New Definition of Humanity."

The man wrote the title in bold print on the center blackboard, at the bottom of a list of ten others, saying the words as he wrote. ". . . OF . . . HU . . . MAN . . . ITY," he said, "MARSHA BAN . . . ER . . . JEE." He looked up. "Anybody else?"

No one spoke.

Leslie leaned toward me. "A new definition of humanity?" she whispered. "Does that sound like . . . ?"

"Yes! But Marsha Banerjee's a *name*," I whispered, "she's a force in artificial intelligence, she's been writing for years. She can't be. . . ."

"I think we're stretching coincidence a little thin," she said. "Look at the other titles!"

Harry Atkin glanced at a note. "The board has asked me to explain that Spring Hill is an intimate gathering of sixty of the most unusual minds they have found in science and communications today." He paused, looked up with a little smile ... that same smile! "Sixty of the most *intelligent* minds is probably a different list. . . ."

Laughter sparkled through the room.

The first topic on the blackboard was Atkin's own:

THE STRUCTURE AND ENGINEERING OF IDEAS.

I turned to Leslie, but she had already read it, nodded as she read on.

"You've been invited because you're different," said Harry, "because the board noticed you skating along on the edge of the ice. Spring Hill was called to put you in touch with a few other skaters as close to the edge as you are. We don't want you to feel alone out there. . . ."

We read the titles on the blackboard, astonishment growing.

FUTURE WITHOUT BORDERS:
THE RISE OF THE ELECTRONIC NATION

EXPERIMENTS IN THE PHYSICS
OF THOUGHT-PARTICLES

WHAT'S A NICE PERSON LIKE YOU
DOING IN A WORLD LIKE THIS?

DESIGNATING TAXES: HOW TO FIND
THE WILL OF THE PEOPLE

WHAT IF: DECISIONS PRE-LIVED

HYPERCONDUCTIVE SUPERCOMPUTERS
IN ECOLOGICAL RESTORATION

INDIVIDUAL PURPOSE:
A THERAPY FOR POVERTY AND CRIME

WAYS TO TRUTH:
WHERE SCIENCE MEETS RELIGION

DESTROYER AS EXPLORER:
NEW ROLES FOR THE MILITARY

CHANGING YESTERDAY, KNOWING TOMORROW

RELATIVES BY CHOICE:
FAMILY IN THE TWENTY-FIRST CENTURY

COINCIDENCE: THE HUMOR OF THE UNIVERSE?

". . . remind you that anyone during any talk," Atkin was
saying, "is encouraged to come to the boards at the side and
write connections, interrelations, directions of research, ideas
that the speaker may have fissioned in our minds. When the
boards are full, erase the idea at the top and add your own,
then the next one down and so on. . . ."

IS DYING NECESSARY?

HOMO AGAPENS:
REQUIREMENTS FOR A NEW RACE

LEARNING DOLPHIN

CREATIVE ALTERNATIVES TO WAR AND PEACE

MANY WORLDS AT ONCE?
SOME PATTERNS OF POSSIBILITY

"Richie, do you see? Look at the last one!"

Atkin took a timer from his pocket, set it off — CHEEP-CHEEP-CHEEP — a demanding electric canary. "Fifteen minutes goes by pretty fast. . . ."

I read, and blinked. Could someone else have found the pattern? We had never stopped to imagine . . . *what if we weren't the only ones who had been there?*

". . . you'll need to skim the surface of your latest work for us as fast as you can," Atkin went on, "what you've been finding, where you're going next. We can get together during the breaks for more detail or to trade research or arrange to meet elsewhere. But you've got to stop when you hear this" — he set off the canary again — "because somebody else has to talk who's just as amazing as you are. Any questions?"

It felt like the start of some big-engine speed dash. We could feel minds running up around us, high-rev exotic things crackling, gnashing to go. Atkin might as well have held a starter's flag.

He turned and checked the clock. "We'll begin in one minute. On the hour. A tape of the meeting will be available. You already have names and numbers for everyone here. Break for lunch at twelve-fifteen, dinner from five to six in the room next door, we'll stop at nine-fifteen tonight, start at eight forty-five again tomorrow. No more questions because I'm the first speaker."

He checked the clock again, a few seconds before the hour, hit the timer.

"Now. Ideas aren't thoughts, they're engineered structure. Notice this and pay attention to the way your ideas are built, and you'll find a dramatic increase in the quality of what you think. You don't believe me? Pick your latest and best idea. Right now, close your eyes and hold that idea in your mind. . . ."

I closed my eyes around what we had learned, that each of us is an aspect of everyone else.

"Look at the idea, and hold up your hand if it seems to you that your idea is made of words." He paused. "Metal?" Another pause. "Empty space?" Pause. "Crystal?"

I raised my hand.

"Open your eyes, please."

I opened my eyes. Leslie's hand was up, and so was the hand of everyone else in the room. There was a murmur of surprise; laughs and ahs and whoas from us all.

"There's a reason it's crystal and there's a reason for the structure that you see," said Atkin. "Every successful idea obeys three rules of engineering. Look for these, and you can tell at once if an idea is going to work for you or if it's going to break down." The room was quiet as sunrise.

"First is the rule of symmetry," he said. "Close your eyes again, and examine the shape of your idea. . . ."

The last time I had felt this way was the last time I had

pushed a jet fighter from full throttle into afterburner, the same burst of wild energy at my back, barely controlled.

As Atkin talked on, a man in the second row stood and walked to the left-side blackboard, wrote swift block letters: DESIGN AND CODE IDEAS COMPUTER-TO-COMPUTER FOR DIRECT WORD-FREE UNDERSTANDING.

Of course, I thought. Word-free! Words are such a crude aid to telepathy. How words had stood in our way when we talked with Pye about time!

"Instead of computer-to-computer, how about mind-to-mind?" Leslie whispered, listening and taking notes at once. "Someday we're going to get around language!"

". . . the fourth rule of any working idea," said Atkin, "is charm. Of the three rules, the fourth is the most important. Yet the only measure for charm is in the. . . ." CHEEP-CHEEP-CHEEP-CHEEP-CHEEP-CHEEP-CHEEP-CHEEP-CHEEP-CHEEP. . . .

From the audience, a groan of frustrated dismay.

Atkin raised his hand to say it's all right, stopped the timer, re-set it, stepped aside. A young man strode forward, speaking even before he reached the microphone.

"Electronic nations are not far-off experiments that may or may not work," he said. "They have already begun, they're already at work, and they exist this moment around us, invisible networks of those who share the same values and ideas, thank you Harry Atkin for opening the way for me so well! The citizens of these nations may be American or

Spanish or Japanese or Latvian, but what holds their unseen countries together is stronger than the borders of any geography. . . ."

The morning was flying by, lightbeams glancing from diamond to emerald to ruby, gaining fire with every shift and turn.

How alone we had felt with our odd thoughts, and what gloriful delight it was to be home with this family of strangers!

"Bless her heart," said Leslie. "Wouldn't little Tink love this, if she could only know?"

"Of course she knows," I whispered. "Where do you think the idea for Spring Hill came from?"

"Didn't she say she was *our* idea fairy, another level of us?"

I touched Leslie's hand. "Where do we stop and the people in this room begin?" I asked.

I didn't know. Where does mind and spirit begin and end, where does caring start and stop, where are the edges of intelligence and curiosity and love?

How many times we'd wished we'd had more bodies! Just a few more bodies, and we could go and stay at once. We could live quietly in wilderness to watch the sun rise in peace, to tame the wildlife, to garden and live close to the earth, and at the same time we could be city-folk crushing into crowds and being crushed by them, seeing films and making them, going to lectures and giving them. We lack enough bodies to meet people every hour and at the same time be alone together, to build bridges and retreats at once, to learn every language, to master every skill, to study and practice and teach everything we'd like to know and do, to work till we drop and to do nothing at all.

". . . found that citizens of these nations forge loyalties to each other that are stronger than loyalty to their geographical countries. This without ever having met in person or even expecting to meet, they grow to love one another for the quality of their thought, their character. . . ."

"These people, they're us in other bodies!" Leslie whispered. "They've always wanted to fly seaplanes, we've done it for them. We've always wanted to talk to dolphins, explore electronic nations, they're doing it for us! People with the same loves aren't strangers, even if they've never met!"

CHEEP-CHEEP-CHEEP- CHEEP-CHEEP-CHEEP-CHEEP-CHEEP-CHEEP-CHEEP. . . .

". . . with the same values aren't strangers," said the young man, stepping away from the microphone, "even if they've never met!"

We glanced at each other, joined a quick round of applause for him, then the next speaker began, leaning her words hard against the clock.

"As the smallest units of matter are pure energy," she said, "so the smallest units of energy may be pure thought. We've made a series of experiments that suggest that the world around us may quite literally be a construction of our thought. We've discovered a particle-like unit which we call the *imajon*. . . ."

Our notebooks were growing thick with pen-wrinkled pages,

every alarm was frustration and promise in one burst of chirps. So much to say, so much to learn! How could so many startling ideas converge in one place?

Could all of us in this room, I thought, be a single person?

I caught Leslie looking at me, turned to meet her eyes. "We do have something to say to them," she said. "Can we live with us if we don't say it?"

I grinned at her. "Dear skeptic."

". . . out of diversity comes this remarkable unity," said the speaker. "We notice so often that what we imagine is exactly what we find. . . ."

As she spoke, I rose and went to the center blackboard, found the chalk, wrote in block letters at the bottom of the list the title of what it was we'd say in our own fifteen minutes.

ONE.

Then I put the chalk down and went back to sit by my wife, to hold her hand. The day had barely begun.

RICHARD BACH

The Bridge Across Forever

The search for love, glittering with Richard Bach's unique, prismatic imagination.

'Did you ever feel that you were missing someone you had never met?'

Haunted by the ghost of the wise, mystical and lovely lady who lives just around the corner in time, Richard Bach begins his quest to find her, to learn of love and immortality not in the hereafter, but in the here and now. Yet caught in storms of wealth and success, disaster and betrayal, he abandons the search, and the wall he builds for protection become his prison. Then he meets the one brilliant and beautiful woman who can set him free, and with her begins a transforming journey, a magical discovery of love and joy.

> 'None . . . can touch Richard Bach for
> his unerring ability to create beauty'
> *San Diego Tribune*

RICHARD BACH

A Gift of Wings

Take flight with this collection of moving short stories from the author of *Jonathan Livingston Seagull*.

These stories, inspired by Bach's lifelong passion for flight, filled with memories of friends from the past and friends not yet met, are woven together with warmth, honesty and courage. With signs and signals, coincidences and tangents turning up at every juncture, Bach shows how truly complex and beautiful life can be, and also how its troubles can in fact knock us onto better paths or teach us lessons we benefit from in other situations. Drawing on the allegorical power of flight, each a mini-parable, these stories will inspire you with their simple experiences made technicolour by the prism of Bach's extraordinary imagination.

Celebrating Richard Bach's unique vision, these transcend their pages to touch the real drama of life with magic that reaches out to us all across its limitless horizons.

RICHARD BACH

Out of My Mind

A radiant flight into the realm of thought and spirit.

This simple, resonant parable about processes of inspiration by the world famous author of *Jonathan Livingston Seagull* tells the story of Bach's discovery of a parallel universe which provides design solutions while we sleep. Puzzling over modifications for his Piper Cub airplane, Bach finds the solutions coming to him 'out of the blue' along with a vision of an unfamiliar woman, but only finds explanations when he yields his spirit to the mystery. He finds himself landing in a strange airfield, and what ensues will delight anyone who has ever marvelled at the capacity of the unconscious mind to find answers to everyday problems.

Out of My Mind is classic Bach, showing his hallmark of reassuringly powerful and affecting writing.

OTHER BOOKS
AVAILABLE FROM PAN MACMILLAN

BUTLER YATES
THE OCULATUM   0 283 07374 8   £6.99

DAVID BLAINE
MYSTERIOUS STRANGER   0 330 41331 7   £12.99

TRICIA STEWART
CALENDAR GIRL   0 330 42738 5   £6.99

All Pan Macmillan titles can be ordered from our website,
www.panmacmillan.com, or from your local bookshop
and are also available by post from:

Bookpost, PO Box 29, Douglas, Isle of Man IM99 1BQ
Credit cards accepted. For details:
Telephone: 01624 677237
Fax: 01624 670923
E-mail: bookshop@enterprise.net
www.bookpost.co.uk

Free postage and packing in the United Kingdom

Prices shown above were correct at the time of going to press.
Pan Macmillan reserve the right to show new retail prices on covers
which may differ from those previously advertised in the text
or elsewhere.